Faith, Love, and Fried Chicken

Four Seasons Set

By Laura J. Marshall

SUMMER

CHAPTER ONE

"Life is too short not to own a convertible." Those words would haunt Jaycee, as far as she could tell, near on all summer now. It was the second time she had found herself broken down on the long windy back road leading from the little store to their house to grab her momma's pop.

She heard the distinctive purr of the truck before she saw him. Dash Matheson. His truck was his baby and that was common knowledge where the townsfolk of Twain, Georgia were concerned. He *would* have to see her stranded....again. He cut the engine and exited the restored 1950 GMC pickup.

"I told ya, Jaycee," he said in his southern drawl, pulling her name out like a yard of fresh taffy at the Culver County Fair.

She was as hot and sticky as taffy too, with the car overheating and the humidity frizzing out her short blonde hair. Her feet ached in her new sandals. Bright red ones with cork heels that matched her toenail polish. Her white shorts showed off tan legs and she had thrown on a plaid cotton shirt of her daddy's over her black tank top.

She turned to face him and tapped her foot.

"Don't you be givin' me a hard time, Dash! I didn't need yer help pickin' her out and I don't need it now."

His slow smile spread up to his eyes. "Now, seein' I own the only mechanic's shop in town, yer gonna have to bring her to me sometime."

Jaycee stamped her foot before she thought better of it, his amusement apparent as he raised his eyebrows fully and leaned against his truck.

He was making it worse. He *always* did! The heat and her temper caused her to sling her purse to the ground and unbutton the long-sleeve shirt.

Removing it with relish, she tied it to her waist. As she straightened, she noticed his smile had been erased and replaced with that dumb look men got at the first sign of female flesh.

"Put them eyes back in yer head and gimme a lift home."

He laughed as she grabbed Momma's pop from the passenger seat and locked the red Chrysler LeBaron convertible's doors. Dash had already slid into his truck and sat tapping his steering wheel.

Jaycee was quiet for a few minutes upon entering the truck cab, anticipating getting home to the AC. She let out long breath. "Gol'durn it, Dash. How can you take this hot truck with no air?"

"What, like your car? Makin' it overheat...and you usin' it with the top down." He laughed.

"Best of both worlds, minus the overheatin' issue."

He waggled his eyebrows her way, flashing a grin meant to charm. "I'll tow her to the shop an' fix her for you."

She considered his offer. He had been the biggest flirt in high school, girls hanging on his arms. He'd been caught kissing under the bleachers so often they gave him the nick name Hot Flash Dash. She wanted to chuckle at that one, but hid her smile by leaning forward to unstick the back of her shoulders from the hot leather seat. *I need my air conditioning.*

"Don't you be makin' things worse. You've been trying to corner me since tenth grade."

"Julia Cozetta Hamilton, that's near on ten years ago. Just 'cuz I didn't catch you doesn't mean I'm still chasin.'"

"Fine. Just fix her. Text me when she's done."

"Will do," he said as he pulled up to the squat ranch house set on the 30 acre farm her family owned. "You workin' tonight?"

"Yes, you know my schedule. Land sakes, it's been the same one since graduation."

"Right. See you at supper then."

Jaycee rolled her eyes, "You need to learn how to cook. Spendin' all yer hard-earned money on Karl's greasy food."

"Better'n what I'd make."

"Truer words," she declared over her shoulder as she exited the truck, slamming the heavy door behind her and tossing her car keys back onto the seat. She sauntered up the walkway, balancing the pop and her purse, trying to appear confident and not twist an ankle.

***

"Dad-blamed shoes," she barked out as she entered the house. She kicked the red heels off with a vengeance as she walked past her brother Marcus lying on the couch. She had bought them online. Good deal too, except they bit into her heels mercilessly. *Cow-poke town, not even big enough for a good shoe store to set up shop.*

"You better watch yer language; Daddy's not in a coddlin' mood," Marcus said, without looking up from his 3DS video game.

"And yer gonna go blind with that thing."

He looked up and caught her eye, crossing his own and laughing. "Too late."

Jaycee continued to the kitchen, dropping her purse along the way as the cool air dried her damp skin. She plopped the two-liter bottle onto the counter next to her mother, who was busy taking cookies out of the oven. The heat hit Jaycee and she retreated to one of the kitchen chairs at the large farmhouse table. She eyed the fresh cookies as her mother slid them onto the cooling rack.

"Lemonade cookies?"

"You know it. Had to triple the batch, gotta have a few to bring to the picnic tomorrow. Can you make some Kool-Aid while I clean up?"

"Momma," Jaycee complained. "Yes, I'll do it." She sighed exasperatedly, remembering the convertible on the side of the road. "Car overheated, back down on Rickett Lane."

"You walk home?" Her mother looked at her from beneath her long blonde bangs as they fell forward across her forehead.

"No. Dash just happened by in that showpiece of his."

"Mighty nice of him. He takin' a look at her for you?"

"Sure enough. Just the trap he's been wantin'."

"Now, Jaycee. You know his aunt Katie is one of my best friends. We've discussed this at length."

"I do not want to be the subject of town gossip, Momma!"

"Well, yer not. And neither is he, just two mother hens passin' the time."

Jaycee made a noncommittal sound and got out the glass pitcher and wooden spoon dyed red from years of Kool-Aid making. She stirred absently after adding the sugar and water, thinking of the cost of the car repair, calculating the expense.

She put the pitcher next to the cookies, grabbing one on the way to her room. *How many more years would she bide her time here?* She plopped onto her unmade bed and reached for absently for a fashion magazine. She paused, contemplating the familiar light yellow walls and floral curtains. A grown woman living at home, stuck in a one diner town. She had plenty tucked away, been waiting on the where to and the why. It hadn't appeared, but Jaycee could feel it blowing across the field in the evening time when she sat on the back porch. A change was coming.

***

Dash tossed the damp towel into the hamper, having just showered off the hot, humid day. He had installed the small shower stall in the back of the shop not long after buying the place off of Old Doug Turner. The pipes generally ran cold, but for him most times this was preferred. Fixing cars was in his blood, but it was hard dirty work.

Wishing he had a piece of land and a family, well that was something he was saving for. And he had his eye on the prize. *Julia Cozetta Hamilton....Jaycee*. He couldn't get her out of his mind...or heart. Sure he had said otherwise, but he knew that to reveal it might push her further away. *Maybe it's time to reveal my intentions; go all in for once.*

Decidedly, he nodded to himself in the mirror, determining to win her affection if it took every heartfelt trick in the book. Good thing it was small town and he knew her routine. Her schedule was as predictable as Mrs. Owen's cat's birthing schedule, filling the small town with orange tabbies for seven years now. One in every farm house and store front. Speaking of which, Casper jumped up and into the sink as Dash finished shaving.

"Gotta go woo yer momma," he whispered conspiringly to the round, purring beast.

He arrived at the diner not long after his regular time and sat at the counter. Marlene brought him a cold Coke poured over lots of crushed ice. He took a long sip and looked over the specials board.

"What's good tonight?"

"The usuals; meatloaf and mashed or pork chops an' the fixins'."

"I'll have the meatloaf. Thanks," he said as he closed the menu. He looked around for Jaycee, spotting her in the lime green Karl's shirt across the room. Even wearing Shrek colors, she caused his heart to stutter.

Marlene caught Dash eyeing Jaycee. Wiping the spot next to him, she slid a fresh paper placemat and napkin-wrapped silverware in front of the empty stool.

"Never gonna happen."

He smiled confidently, a plan forming in his head. Turning to face the counter, he gave her a winning smile, "It's only a matter of fried chicken."

Marlene smiled at his answer, then raised an eyebrow.

"What's only a matter of fried chicken?" Jaycee repeated. She came to stand near Dash with her hand on her hip.

He took a long pull on the pop and braced his two hands against the counter, turning and leaning over in his stool so his eyes were level with Jaycee's.

"You and me," he said slowly, letting his lips roll over the words as they carried to her on a breath and sank against the softness of her cheeks. Her beautiful light-green eyes narrowed and her full lashes fell in quick succession as she blinked rapidly.

"Y-you and me? And fried chicken?"

"That's right, darlin'."

"Don't you darlin' me, Dash. I know what comes after your 'darlin'. Sure enough, I'm in your sights, but I'm leaving this town, not stayin' and settin' up a Mom and Pop with you."

Marlene had wandered away once she saw Jaycee's temper flare. Jaycee was but three inches from his face. His gaze lazed on her lips and then swiftly found her eyes again.

"Don't let the future overwhelm the moment," he whispered quietly. He reached for her hand, just running his thumb across the top of it and then let it go.

She stood there speechless. He saw her find her feet again when Eileen Casey yelled over the supper din for Jaycee to run for some napkins, since little Kenny spilled his milk across the table. He gazed at her retreating back and sat up straighter on the stool. Silence being an uncommon response, it gave him a glimmer of hope.

CHAPTER TWO

It was going on nine o'clock when Jaycee walked out the front door of the diner. She sat for a moment on the step, sliding her feet out of the worn tennis shoes and yanking off her socks. The cool concrete soothed her tired, aching feet. Across the empty parking lot, Dash leaned against the driver's door of her convertible. She met his gaze and he smiled, dangling her keys from one finger.

"Took ya' long enough," she yelled, trying to sound more confident and carefree than she felt. Truth was, he had gotten to her earlier; his intense gaze and his lips so close to her own. She didn't know what to think of him and this persistence of his. She was beginning to feel flattered and just a bit curious. *Oh, Jaycee….you know what happened to the cat.*

She walked towards him slowly, moving from the concrete sidewalk and into the gravel lot.

Forgetting her bare feet, she winced unexpectedly. Dash cut the distance between them in long strides and without so much as a "by your leave" swept her into his arms.

He stood there for a moment, silently looking down at her in the moonlight. She was struck dumb by the feel of his hard muscles around her and the scent of his cologne...and a distinctly Dash scent. The scent of a man.

"What do ya' think yer doin?"

"Rescuin' my lady."

He grinned down at her and mock-staggered back to the car, feigning a burden. He opened the car door with the hand beneath her and slid her in behind the steering wheel. Leaning across her, he fit the key into the ignition.

"Your chariot."

"H-how much do I owe you?"

"Let's just say, you eat with me tomorrow...at the church picnic."

She considered him in the still night with nary a car passing by and with only the tree frogs for music.

"Dash...."

He put his finger to her lips, still bent to her level. "Tomorrow. We'll talk tomorrow. Promise me you'll come?"

Her mind had blanked at his touch, so she whispered, "I-I'll be there."

He eased out a slow smile, lighting up the space around him, and shut the driver's door. He motioned for her to fasten her seatbelt and she obeyed without a word, wondering at her own timidity. Flipping on the lights, she eased the car out of the space and then saw an image that would consume her until she fell into a restless sleep later that night: Dash reflected in her rearview mirror, red from her taillights, looking heartbreakingly romantic.

***

Jaycee rolled over and with bleary eyes looked at the clock. The blue numbers glowed back at her, 7:30. She groaned as she grabbed her phone from the nightstand to see who was texting her this early. Kitty. Again waking her up at the crack of dawn; well, Jaycee's dawn.

She rolled onto her back, flipping through the consecutive texts.

I'm still waitin.

Let me know.

Can't wait 2 cu.

She grinned and tapped a reply back. *Soon. Mayb nxt wk. Let u know 2mrrw.*

She hit send and got a reply a moment later.

Kk. Happy 4th!

The 4th of July! Jaycee had forgotten. The church picnic was that afternoon...and Dash. She had promised to eat with him.

Having lost sleep the night before, she buried her head beneath the pillow, reveling in its coolness. On the cusp of a light sleep, she heard her phone beep. *Kitty, no doubt.*

She reached a hand from beneath her covers, fumbling for the phone and knocking a magazine to the floor. She finally clasped the cool plastic, letting out a triumphant sound. *Kitty Ames.* Her best friend since Junior High. *Inseparable.* That is, until she had left for New York not long after graduating. She worked for *Acclaim* Magazine now, copyediting. Had herself set up in a nice apartment with a male roommate and a chic lifestyle. She basically hounded Jaycee daily to move there. It was about time she planned it. A week's visit; a trial run. She missed Kitty, who didn't come home near as often as Kitty's mom would like since she and her dad had divorced.

Jaycee glanced down at the phone. The screen flashed Dash's name and a short text.

Need ur help.

That was different. She texted back with deft fingers. *Me?*

Yes! Flashed back and a moment later, *Can u come?*

Her breath released in a hiss. Did he mean now?

At the picnic, you mean?

No. I need ur help. My house.

She texted back before she thought better of it. *Kk.*

Tossing the phone onto the bed, she headed for the bathroom, flipping on the shower water to hot and coming back to rummage through her bureau.

Too many morning people in my life.

***

Dash was glad Jaycee was up. He had been since six o'clock, digging through the boxed-up contents of his parent's house deposited into the spare room of his rental house several years ago. He hadn't had the heart to go through everything. He finally found what he had been looking for; his mother's wicker picnic basket. A red-checkered tablecloth had been stuffed inside. It smelled of mold so he threw that into the trash can and hosed out the basket. It presently sat upended in the middle of his front lawn airing out.

After that task, he had swilled down a good amount of black coffee with Casper eyeing him suspiciously over the early morning ruckus. He then pulled out the two chickens from the fridge. He read the sticker in the early morning light. *Fryer.* He was almost sure he had gotten the right thing. He cut the plastic packaging away and put the scrawny, slippery birds on a plate.

Washing his hands, he went to the kitchen table and flipped open his laptop, searching through a few dozen recipes and, deciding on the three best candidates, printed them off. *I have no clue. None whatsoever. What was I thinking? Those*

stories, the ones grandma used to tell me about
when she and grandpa fell in love, that's what.

And so he'd texted her. As dumb as he felt
doing it, she was going to be eating too and he
didn't know how to wrangle those slimy bones and
skin into any semblance of chicken parts he
recognized.

He heard a knock at the door and there she
stood; fresh from a shower and as flustered as a
dog chasing its tail for too long. She pushed her
way past him when he opened the door, her
perfume floating past him on the air.

"What's yer emergency?"

Before he could answer her, she was in the
kitchen. *Women's intuition.* He followed behind, his
head hanging low. Seeing Casper slinking behind
him as if expecting a show, Dash rolled his eyes at
the cat before facing Jaycee.

She stood there in her pink terrycloth shorts
and Twain high school T-shirt, tapping her pink
Converse-covered toe. He glanced at her face, the

overhead light catching the shimmer of her lip gloss, those lips shining just for him. He stared, mesmerized, as he spoke.

"Chicken," he said, nodding towards the island countertop.

"Is this about that crazy idea of yours yesterday...you and me and fried chicken? What're you tryin' to pull?" She said, wariness in her voice as she glanced at the raw birds.

"Now, I just had the idea of makin' a nice picnic meal and then realized, I don't know what to do with them." His chin lifted. "The birds."

She giggled then. "And I'm your rescue?"

"That's the plan. Rescue us both from a trip to County Hospital."

This made her laugh harder and she wiped tears from her eyes.

"Must we do this at eight am?"

"Picnics in a few hours' time."

Jaycee moved to the sink and washed her hands. "Cutting board?"

He grinned his thanks and went to remove it from a cupboard.

"I need a fresh plate and a sharp knife too...please."

He went to work getting her everything she required and stood near the counter, waiting for his next order and trying to avoid the sight of those birds. He could still remember the cold, wet, bony feel against his hands. A shiver ran up his spine.

"Afraid of a little raw meat?" She chided him, quickly working with the sharp knife and creating the familiar pieces he had grown up eating: *Breast, wing, drumstick.*

"No, I just never realized chickens were so....gross." He laughed at his own words and went over to the coffeepot. "You want a cup?"

"Sure. You have any flavored creamer?"

"No," he said, but suddenly had an idea. "I have amaretto and chocolate syrup. Let me make you a *frou-frou* coffee."

"Sounds divine."

He passed behind her, removing items from a cabinet over the stove and from the refrigerator. It didn't take Jaycee long to finish cutting up the two chickens into a neat pile before her on the plate. She washed the knife, cutting board, and her hands in hot soapy water. Dash eyed her triumphantly as he slid the coffee in front of her as she sat down at the kitchen table.

She fingered through the recipes he had printed earlier and took her first sip. She looked at him with appreciation on her face as he sat across from her. "*Dee-licious.*"

"Thank you. And thanks for helping with the chicken."

She assessed him over her next sip and he couldn't help but warm under her gaze. She looked so good sitting in his kitchen, the cat lounging near the AC vent in the floor and the morning sunlight streaming through the large bay window.

"You know how to fry chicken?"

"Um, no. But I've got those recipes."

"One of these calls to fryin' in shortening. You know how to do that?"

"Oh, I-I didn't notice."

He could tell she was holding in a grin.

"Tell you what," she said, "I'll fry up the chicken usin' my Momma's recipe and you go to the store for the rest of what we need for the picnic."

"Such as?"

Her eyes lit up and she pushed her empty cup towards him.

"Surprise me."

CHAPTER THREE

Jaycee parked her car and raised the ragtop. She was proud of herself. She had made two different coatings from the meager ingredients in Dash's kitchen, frying the pieces to perfection. She'd tasted one of the last to come out of the hot oil; it was crispy and juicy, just like her Momma's. She had grown up in the kitchen at Momma's elbow, knowing most of her recipes by heart, fried chicken being one of them.

She entered the house and headed towards her room, intent on a cool shower. She turned over in her mind the clothes in her closet, deciding what to wear to the picnic.

"Jaycee?"

"Yes, Daddy?" she called from the hallway, a hand on her doorknob.

"Come see me, please."

Her daddy's voice sounded congenial. 'Course, it being July 4th, he'd be taking it easy except to care for the animals.

She found him in the living room seated in his favorite chair, remote in hand. At his elbow was the ever-present bag of French-fried onions, her daddy's favorite snack. Momma bought them in big, resealeable bags from the local bulk warehouse. Who in tarnation invested in French-fried onions like the Hamilton family was beyond Jaycee. They were meant for green bean casserole, not every day fare.

She approached him, kissing his cheek and smelling the familiar onion scent.

"Where ya been?"

"Just helpin' fry some chicken for the picnic."

"You?" His left eyebrow went up.

"I can cook, Daddy."

"I assumed you could; just haven't seen you do much 'round here."

She took a seat on the couch, glancing at the NASCAR pre-show on TV.

"Exceptin' Momma's birthday, you know how she is about her kitchen."

He nodded, catching her eye and grinning, "Shoulda' been a chef."

"She is, Daddy; your own personal one."

He laughed at that and patted his slightly rounded middle. "That she is."

They sat in comfortable silence, Jaycee trying to decide if it was a good time to talk about New York. "Been talkin' to Kitty," she began.

"Yeah? She home for the 4th?"

"No." Jaycee bit her lip in anticipation, the rest coming out in a rush. "You know I've been savin'. I'm gonna go up there for a week; check things out."

Her father's eyes slid from the TV and met her own. "When's this?"

"Week after next. I'll get off work."

"And then what?"

Jaycee shrugged then regretted it. She sat up tall on the couch and stuck her chin out. "Then we'll see. If I like it, I'm goin' to live there."

He stared at her hard. As the minutes passed, his expression softened and he beckoned her closer. She came to perch on the heavy rolled arm of his chair. He put his hand on her back and rubbed it gently.

"I trust your judgment, Julia Cozetta Hamilton. You go and follow yer dreams. Decide what you want out of life and go get it."

Tears sprung to her eyes and she turned and flung her arms around his neck, loving her father for the simplicity of his speech and the way he always spoke to her from his heart.

"I will, Daddy. I will."

****

Dash arrived at Jaycee's house at two o'clock. He wiped his palms across his khaki shorts, nervousnes***

The entire town of Twain, Georgia seemed to be at Trinity Church's annual picnic. It was one of two churches in town that held a July 4th celebration, which ended over at Moonlight Lake with the county fireworks.

s causing his stomach to flutter even though he had seen her a few hours earlier. He rang the doorbell, expecting Mr. or Mrs. Hamilton to answer. He was pleasantly surprised when the green-painted door swung in and Jacyee stood there with her mouth curved up in greeting. In her turquoise sundress, she took his breath away.

"You look beautiful," he said as he drew the bouquet of wildflowers from behind his back.

"Well, aren't these lovely; you're lookin' a fine sight yourself, Dash."

He momentarily preened under her scrutiny and then lifted a hand, self-consciously checking the cowlick at the side of his head.

"I'll put these in water. They won't last long in this heat."

He nodded and followed her into the house. He stood just inside the door as he heard a cabinet open and the water run briefly. She returned a moment later, a yellow cotton sweater and a covered-plate in hand. She wiggled the sweater.

"For later, during the fireworks; lotsa bugs."

"Right," he said.

"And dessert." She jiggled the plate.

He reached for it so she could grab her purse and lock the door. "Nice." He held the plate up to his nose to sniff the contents.

"Dash! You wait 'til later. It's a surprise."

He grinned at her over the plate. "It certainly is."

They arrived in Dash's truck, causing a stir among the menfolk, many of who surrounded the truck as he exited. Jaycee could almost feel the air hanging heavy with whispers from the women on the lawn as she waited for him at the front of the truck. He disentangled himself from the conversation and joined her with the picnic basket in hand.

"Shall we?" He led the way onto the grass next to the large church and past a covered tent with a line of tables laden with food. More tables were set up for bingo and face painting. He reached for Jaycee's hand as bathing-suit clad kids ran past and through dueling sprinklers. They continued walking until he stopped beneath a large oak tree. Its limbs stretched wide and proud with plenty of shade beneath its branches.

He let loose of her hand and set the picnic basket down, producing a plastic-encased red and white checked tablecloth. Unwrapping the new purchase, he spread it on the ground.

He gestured for her to sit, which she did without hesitation, anticipating Dash's first taste of her fried chicken. She stretched her legs out and kicked off her white sandals.

He bent his legs beneath him as he dug a hand into the basket, producing two chilled sweet teas.

"Let's cool down a bit before we eat. Guess we shoulda taken yer car," he said sheepishly.

"It's okay. I woulda' let you drive, though."

He smiled at that. She knew she was like a momma lion with her cub where her car was concerned. She could still remember how he had advised her against the purchase while eating supper one night at the diner. She had pointedly ignored his advice and continued to charm Mrs. Brewer. The car had sat in the old woman's garage going on 10 years and Jaycee had finally sweet-talked her into selling.

He tapped his glass bottle to hers. "Happy July 4th."

"Happy July 4th," she grinned. "Thanks for inviting me before I...." Her voice trailed off.

"Before you what?" he questioned, taking a sip of tea.

"I'm goin' to visit Kitty."

His eyebrows arched, wrinkling his forehead. "In New York?"

"Yes." She held her breath for a moment, then willed it out in small fractions as he responded.

"Ahh, nice. For how long?"

"For a week and then...maybe to stay."

He had been mid-sip and she saw him swallow hard with a cough.

"Wow."

"I've been savin' since graduation. Don't know what for, but I think this is it."

"*Think* this is it?" She heard the weight of the question in his voice.

"My life's not all mapped out, Dash." She felt her face start to redden and her temper rise.

"It didn't come with an instruction manual. I've been workin' at the same job since high school. It's — it's downright suffocatin'."

She could almost see his thoughts turning, anticipating his disapproval before it came.

"And so's this town," she finished.

There. She'd said it. Laid it out for him. Why she cared to explain to him she couldn't fathom. *Hot Flash Dash.* How dare he tug at her heart with those dark green eyes of his. With a chin held-fast with yesterday's scruff, making him appear rugged and capable...and downright attractive. He hadn't said a thing since her outburst.

She sighed and lay back onto the cloth, the iced tea wet in her hand at her side. She imagined she could feel the swaying from the branches up and through the tree's roots in the ground. She stared at the thick, crooked limbs above their heads, breathing in the familiarity of the church and its old trees.

She felt him lie down. Her tension eased. This was silly. She put way too much pressure on herself. *Should've kept my mouth shut.* She had probably just ruined their picnic. And she didn't know why it mattered as much as it did, but her heart hurt and her eyes stung with tears.

***

Dash kept quiet for what seemed like a long stretch of time. He eased his legs out straight, silently saying a prayer and feeling a slight breeze wash over him. The sounds of the picnic farther down the lawn continued.

Feeling a strange, cold, damp feeling near his elbow, he sat up. Seeing the source, he gulped and looked over at Jaycee's serene face.

"Jaycee?"

"Mmmmhmmm?"

"We need to eat. I-I, the picnic basket's leakin'."

He saw her screw her face up, trying to figure that one out. She opened one eye to look up at him.

"Leakin'? What have you done now?"

He grinned sheepishly down at her. "The ice cream..."

"Ice cream!" she interrupted, sitting up quickly.

"Made some homemade, last night late. Vanilla and honey. Thing is, I filled the bottom of the basket with ice and...and it's meltin' everywhere."

She scrambled up onto her knees and scooted over to the basket, seeing the water stain at the cloth's edge. Opening the lid and peering in, she fell onto her side, laughing loudly.

Dash couldn't help but join in as he thought of his brilliant idea, not taking into account the extreme heat of the day.

"Quit laughin' at me and help me eat the ice cream. It'll be thawin' next."

He removed two Tupperware bowls and some plastic spoons from the hamper and held one out to a recovering Jaycee. As they began eating, Jolene and Dee came over to the tree. They plopped on the edge of the tablecloth simultaneously.

"Well, ain't this a surprise," Dee said in greeting.

Dash nodded in return, filling his mouth with the deliciously cool treat. He wanted to get to Jaycee's fried chicken and ate his ice cream in fast spoonfuls.

"Hey there," Jaycee said, offering no explanation. She closed her eyes briefly in seeming enjoyment after each bite. She faced Dash. "You made this all by yourself?"

"I *do* have my talents," he said, pleased she liked it.

She grinned back and wiggled her toes.

"How's your summer goin'," she asked the newest arrivals.

Jolene spoke first, waving her hand and flashing a ring with suitable dramatic flair. "Todd and I got engaged," she squealed delightedly.

Dash watched Jaycee's reaction to the announcement. She looked at the ring and into Jolene's face. Jolene had always been a sweet girl, since high school, kind and shy. It was Dee's influence that made Dash wince when he saw her coming. Dee always seemed to have Jolene under her thumb and by the expression on Dee's face, she didn't look too thrilled.

"I'm so happy for you. Todd is a great guy and what a ring!" Jaycee oohed and ahhed at the diamond. Jolene drew closer to Jaycee, sharing the plans she had made so far for the wedding.

Dee stared at the pair then sidled closer to Dash. Beneath the chatter, she questioned him, "So...you two an item?"

"We're just sharin' a meal together, Dee. Nothin' more."

"Seems pretty cozy to me, Flash."

He groaned inwardly. She always knew how to get on his last nerve. "That was high school. Time to move on."

"Well...it's somethin' I'll never forget," she said, tracing a hand up Dash's arm.

He turned and looked her square in the face, meeting her eyes as he spoke. "It was a kiss. Just one. I was a bit too loose in my youth. Sorry to lead you along."

"Whatev'. Water under the bridge," Dee laughed and loudly added so the other two could hear, "or under the stadium bleachers, I should say. Oh, memories."

He rolled his eyes at her and announced loudly, "Well, I invited Jaycee to eat with me and we've got to get to the meal. The ice is sure meltin' fast." He indicated the puddle of water and mud beneath the picnic basket that had been shifted onto the grass.

CHAPTER FOUR

Jaycee watched Dash as he took his first bite of chicken. It was always better when it sat in the fridge and got cold for a few hours. She smiled as satisfaction settled over his features.

"What'dya think?" For some reason it was important to hear him say he liked it.

He finished chewing the bite, dramatically lengthening his chews, then patting his lips with a napkin. "Will you marry me?"

"Good gravy," she said, pleased with his ribbing. *A lifetime of meals; that's a high compliment.*

"It's the best chicken I've ever tasted. Better'n Grandma's. 'Course she's not here to clock me for that one." He smiled and met her gaze.

A short time later their bellies were full and only a few pieces remained. They both agreed the Cajun spice coating was the best.

Dash dumped out the last of the ice and placed the covered plate with Jaycee's mystery dessert back into the hamper. Packing up their spot, they wandered over by the tent and tables. The hottest part of the day had passed and a light breeze blew across the field.

Jaycee spied her parents and they went over to say hello. Her father stood chatting with Clint Sparrow and his son Todd. The Sparrows owned the local hardware and feed store. Jaycee interrupted the conversation on the varieties of protein-based cattle feed to plant a kiss on her father's cheek. Her mother sat nearby with Katie and Dash slid into a chair next to his aunt.

Jaycee took a seat near her mother. At the other end of the table, Cora Tubbins sat with her newborn baby atop the table in its carrier. She had two toddlers at her side. Jaycee smiled and nodded toward the newest Tubbins family member. "Congratulations. She's beautiful."

"Thanks, sweetie." Cora looked up briefly from the paper plate in front of her as she cut her children's hotdogs into small pieces.

"Can I help?" Jaycee offered.

Cora smiled wearily but grinned at each of her children with pride, "We're fine. The twins are learnin' patience in little ways and are being great big brothers."

Mike Tubbins came up behind his wife, placing a plate filled with watermelon on the table near the baby. He rubbed her back briefly and reached for the sleeping infant.

"Now don't you wake her."

He beamed, lifting the tiny bundle up and onto his shoulder. "Thought I'd take her into the coolness of the church for a spell."

"Don't you fall asleep on a pew in there," his wife scolded, smiling.

His quiet laugh carried back to Jaycee and she averted her eyes as she saw a tender look pass between the two.

***

Dash drove the truck through the woods and up the dirt road that led to Moonlight Lake. A line of cars stretched before and behind them. He drove into the dirt lot overgrown with weeds, backing in so the truck bed faced the lake.

"Perfect viewin' spot," he said, as he jumped from the truck, grabbing a bag from between them on the seat.

Jaycee slid from the high truck seat as a car pulled next to them. She waved at Maude and Flint Nolan as they exited their car.

"Fine night."

"Indeed," she responded with a smile.

When she reached the back of the truck, she saw Dash had spread a blanket in the bed with the tailgate down.

"Figure we'd have our dessert." He hinted again at Jaycee's treat. "Then we'll head down to the lake."

She nodded. The sun had set but the sky was still light enough to see by. Puffy white clouds lazed as the moon became the center of attention. "Poor moon."

"Hmmm?"

"Going to be outdone by the pyrotechnics."

"A momentary flash can never outshine its constancy and beauty, being a light in the darkness."

They looked at each other, sitting side-by-side in the truck bed.

"You continue to surprise me," she said, marveling at this side of him. It must be so nice to be assured and confident. To know exactly what you are and where you want to be.

"As do you, Jaycee. Yet, I've been aware of your worth, intelligence, and wit now for years.

Just couldn't get close enough to wear down yer suspicions."

"Suspicions?" she repeated. So he had known she was wary. Been that way since high school, always skirting him and his offers of friendship and attempts at deeper conversation.

He smiled. *She knew that he knew that she knew*. What a thought, let alone a mouthful. She remained quiet instead of voicing an excuse.

Slowly the traffic eased in the lot. Stragglers walked past them and they waved *hellos* at neighbors and friends. Down near the water, they could see families sitting lakeside, others standing. The boats on the horizon took on the appearance of shadows as night deepened.

"My turn for a surprise." Jaycee reached into the basket and pulled out the foil-covered plate. "Close yer eyes." She hadn't planned to say that. *Honest to sweet cherry pie*, she hadn't. But she couldn't resist.

52

As he sat there with a slight grin and his eyes closed, she moved closer. Close enough to feel the warmth of the arm at his side and his leg as it hung over the lowered liftgate.

"Open yer mouth," she whispered, close to his ear.

His smile disappeared and he fidgeted a moment, almost as if he was about to reach for her.

A thread of disappointment lit through her. It disappeared as she realized the power she had with his eyes shut. She could *kiss* him. Her stomach flipped in reaction to the thought and she hesitated.

"Good Lord, woman. You are the biggest tease," he said. "I better not choke on a bug."

She laughed softly. "Stop spoilin' my fun. Open," she insisted.

She dangled the strawberry near his mouth, causing him to arch his neck and reach and just feel the edge of it close to his lips. The smooth white chocolate dipped strawberry with a ring of blue sparkle-sugar descended. He opened his eyes as he took the first bite.

"Delicious," he said, when he had finished chewing.

"July 4th berries. My specialty."

"I'm surprised Marcus didn't eat them all on you."

"He would've too if I hadn't hid some in the barn fridge."

"I know it." He smacked his lips. "He's a good kid. Stops by to help around the shop once in awhile."

"Our Marcus?" *Well miracles abound, he did lift his head from his games now and again.*

"Yeah," he said, grabbing for another strawberry off the plate.

She took one herself and eased back in the truck, then rolled onto her belly on the blanket, adjusting her dress and sweater.

He followed suit, the plate of berries at their elbows between them.

"You wanna go closer or is this okay?"

"I like it here," she said quietly.

"Me too." He reached over then and touched her arm. "Hey, I wanted to thank you for comin'...for everything."

"Was a mighty fine 4th. Thank *you*." She wanted to say more. Ask him his dreams and plans; get to know more of Dash. The essence of him. He was in her senses. His deep southern voice and easy smile; the tilt of his head when he spoke.

Laughter of the townsfolk down by the lake carried. Jaycee stared into the crowd, seeing the sputter of sparklers and hearing the first test shots firing across the lake. Things quieted momentarily in anticipation of the celebration.

She was anticipating – not New York City, not seeing Kitty, or the possibility of a big move from rinky-dink Twain, Georgia – but *him*. She was anticipating Dash and his soft, strong lips on hers.

And as her breath caught at the thought and the first fireworks lit up the night sky, he did it.

He kissed Julia Cozetta Hamilton *but good and sound* right there in the back of his truck across a plate of her famous July 4th berries…and she liked it.

***

It was a cool morning. Earlier than usual for Jaycee to be up and about. She found her mother on the screened in back porch, coffee in hand.

"Mornin', Momma."

"Good morning, Peaches."

Jaycee warmed at the familiar nickname. She plopped herself into a floral pad-covered chair and stretched her arms over her head.

"Need to talk to you."

"I heard. Daddy told me." Her mother's glistening eyes found her own and Jaycee could see the worry there. "New York? The *city*?"

"I've been savin'. You knew it would come eventually. Me leavin'." She hesitated, not as confident after that kiss and holding Dash's hand the rest of last night. He had walked her to the door and hugged her firmly, capturing her in a hard embrace. But as she had tipped her mouth up to his, he had kissed the tip of her nose, and followed it by a chuck under the chin.

".....A pipe dream," her mother finished saying, interrupting her thoughts.

"I'll work and decide who and what I want to be. No more Twain aspirations of only bein' a wife and momma."

Jaycee's mother visibly winced and tried to smile, shrugging a shoulder.

"No offence, Momma," She grabbed her mother's hand as it lay in her lap. "I love you. I-I just need to know where *I* fit." She was so confused, now more than ever.

Her mother nodded slowly. "I know you do, Peaches. I know you do."

CHAPTER FIVE

As sure as the poplar tree leaves turn when a big rain is about to come, Dash had wanted to kiss Jaycee when he dropped her off after the fireworks. He knew she wanted him to, but something in him told him to wait. She needed to ponder her own feelings and direction without any more influence by him. He was sure. She was his. He couldn't see himself with another girl and hadn't for a long while, but...his heart felt vulnerable. And he had no one he trusted with it to talk to.

Aunt Katie. He had shared about Jaycee over the years, but to reveal this much, and her being so close to Jaycee's mother....*she* wouldn't do.

No, this was between him and God...and Jaycee. And the good Lord knew Dash couldn't talk to her. Not *yet*.

She had some major decisions to make and he had just complicated her life even more. At least he *hoped* he had.

***

"Problem is, Julia Cozetta Hamilton, you are spoiled."

She stood there in her customary pose, hands on her hips, her ire rising. Her Vera Bradley duffel bag sat on the splintered wood of the rail station walkway. Her train was due to depart in fifteen minutes.

"Dash, you've had all week to accost me with yer sorry self and you choose to show up now?"

"I knew you were leavin', just not...not this week. You didn't give me much of a chance." His voice trailed off.

"Sadie was takin' off next week. It happened quick."

"Three days ago. Three days isn't that long, Jaycee. I was comin' in tonight for supper."

She huffed out a long breath, "Well, enjoy yer meatloaf. I won't be there."

"Now, let's not leave off like this. I-I wanted to say somethin'."

She looked around at the two people standing at the other end of the walk. Waves of heat shimmered off the ground. "I'm listenin'."

Dash stepped closer and took her hand, "I guess I'm not much good for words or speakin' from my heart." He visibly gulped and with his free hand, loosened his collar.

She could've laughed if he didn't appear so jittery or if she didn't feel that this was somehow a moment where life slowed down and paused. She ached to ease his nervousness.

She pulled him to within inches of her and a crooked smile appeared, dancing at the corner of his mouth. Butterflies flew about her stomach at his nearness and she breathed out, "You know, you've had me waitin' on you *all week*."

"Three days, Jaycee."

"I know. I've been countin'."

"You didn't answer my texts."

"I was packin' and doin' laundry. Momma had half the county in sayin' goodbye. You'd think I was goin' away for a lifetime."

"*Are you?*"

It was her turn to gulp, her palms growing sweaty. "I don't know. I'm confused. Maybe goin' will help."

"Have you prayed about it?"

"Some."

"And?"

"And they're hittin' the ceilin', Dash. Flyin' back down in my face."

"They're not. The answer will come. Go. Have fun. Give Kitty my best."

"I'll see you in a week."

"Rightly so. Text me if you need anything."
He said as he looked down into her eyes, "I'd come,
you know."

"You do the same. I'd-I'd come too."

He smiled. Her world seemed to tilt. His
breath fell across her lashes. "Thank you."

He gently captured her lips with his own.
Tracing a finger down her cheek, he lengthened the
kiss. His hand moved to the back of her neck,
gently massaging small circles.

He pulled away. An emptiness descended
around her, the air hanging with the void. Before
Jaycee could open her eyes, he was gone.

***

Jaycee arrived in New York City half a day
later. She was unsure of where she was at any
given moment, zipping as fast as they were through
large cities with tall buildings and small towns with
long wheat blowing in the night sky that reminded

her of Twain. She had slept half the time and looked out the window the rest as night turned back into day.

They pulled underground and into Penn Station. She emerged from the train and looked around at the throngs of people. Grasping her bag close to her shoulder, she wrinkled her nose at the odd smells in the tunnel. It was with relief that she heard a familiar voice.

"Hey, Peaches," Kitty called loudly over the noise, running up next to her. Jaycee found herself in a warm embrace.

"Peaches, is it?" She heard a distinctly male voice question over Kitty's shoulder.

"John," Kitty said triumphantly, turning with Jaycee still held in her embrace, "This is Jaycee."

Jaycee nodded and smiled in response to John's amused greeting. So this was Kitty's roommate. She kept the million questions forming in her mind to herself as she saw the handsome, dark-haired young man standing by them. He wore sharply-creased, straight-leg khakis with a fashionable white polo.

As he stepped towards the pair, he reached out a hand, "Here let me help." He took the duffel bag from her without waiting for an answer and started walking towards the stairs behind him. They caught up to him and fell into step as Kitty gushed over how great Jaycee looked.

It wasn't long before they were out into the bustling city. John hailed a cab and Jaycee turned in circles as she stood next to the busy street. Large buildings surrounded her on every side each with hundreds of windows and the occasional electronic billboard flashing colorful images. If the heat of Georgia could be described as humid and sticky, New York's summer swelter felt unrelenting as it bounced off the pavement. A heavy cloud cover seemed to hang over the city and the sun struggled for center stage. A cab pulled up a moment later and John threw her bag into the trunk. The three of them stuffed themselves into the back seat in relief as the air conditioning cooled their flushed faces.

***

Kitty and Jaycee sat cross-legged on Kitty's bed. John had offered to grab Chinese for dinner with a plan for them to head out to some nightlife later.

"Ten o'clock?" Jaycee questioned.

"Yeah, sometimes not 'til eleven, but we thought we'd ease you into things."

Jaycee laughed. She was like an alien on another plant. "I can't wait." She glanced around, seeing Kitty's door open and then remembered John had left the tiny apartment.

"So, tell me...are you and John an item? I didn't get that impression from you, but...you were never one to pass up a gorgeous man."

"He is, isn't he? And sweet as yesterday's sweet tea. There's just no chemistry. Like my big brother."

"*Come on*, Kitty!"

"God's honest truth." Kitty held up her hand in silent pledge. "I thought you two...you know, might hit it off."

"My head's spinnin'. I wouldn't know right from wrong right now. Especially with Dash and his southern courtin' ways."

"You didn't say much. What's going on? I knew he fancied you."

Jaycee reddened as she thought back to Dash's kisses, her heart skipping a beat. "I like him. Enough to ponder what I'm doin' here."

"He'll be there when you get back. Things don't change quickly in Twain, Georgia."

****

Karl's had lost some of its appeal without Jaycee there to season the meal. Dash got back to his house in record time from supper and flopped onto the living room couch. He flipped open his phone. No texts. Jaycee must've arrived earlier in the day, safe and sound by now. With his phone open, he weighed calling Dave or Chuck to go for a beer and play some darts.

He flipped it closed a moment later. He knew he wasn't good company and if he wasn't the regular jokester he was known to be, his buddies would be wondering. *Too many questions he wasn't ready to answer.*

Casper jumped up next to him, rubbing her face against his hand. She occasionally looked up and past him into the kitchen. He had fed her earlier, but she was a beggar.

"Yeah, I know what you *really* want."

He rubbed her briskly behind her ears until she was putty in his hands, rolling onto her side and showing her furry, fat stomach.

"Have you no shame?" He laughed softly.

The cat looked at him through her slitted eyes, purring loudly. He absently thought he heard a crackling in the kitchen. *Fridge making ice.*

Dash reached over his silly putty cat and grabbed the remote from the coffee table. He settled himself lower, his head against a couch cushion. She snuggled in closer as he whispered softly, flicking through channels, "Just you and me tonight, beautiful."

CHAPTER SIX

The little black dress clung to Jaycee like a second skin. It was Kitty's, along with the strappy heels on her feet. As teens they had always exchanged clothes, so it was only natural for Kitty to advise her on her clubbing attire.

She emerged behind Kitty and followed her to the kitchen. John's eyes grew large and round as they fell on Jaycee as she stepped into the room. He let out a low whistle and stepped closer, offering her a glass of wine.

"Peaches," He said quietly, his voice low.

Jaycee heard Kitty's laughter, "I told ya' to hold onto your teeth, John."

"You are dan-ger-ous." He teased. "I'll stay close for crowd control," he said with a wink.

John's hair was slicked back and he appeared fresh from a shower. He caught her green eyes with his own bright blue ones and held them for a moment longer than Jaycee was comfortable with. She looked away and faked a sip of the wine in her hand. She wasn't much of a drinker.

Kitty stood across the kitchen in a red dress with a ruffle at the bottom and matching heels that showed off her long legs.

"Wish I had a tan like you," Kitty lamented.

"The benefits of the farm and a convertible," she said, grinning.

"You live on a farm?" John questioned.

"Sure enough. We raise cattle, chickens, have a few horses, and peach trees. Daddy's all for tryin' a little of this and that."

"Daddy?" He smirked over the rim of his glass.

Kitty teased. "That's what we all call our parents down south, not this "mother and father" you Northerners use."

He looked at Jaycee with even more interest, "I've lived in the city my whole life. Sounds like heaven."

"I guess if your idea of heaven includes dirt, smelly animals, and manure," she said without thinking.

John studied her quietly, "So – you here to see the great big world?"

"I am." She put her glass on the counter and tugged the hem of her dress down slightly.

John's eyebrows raised incrementally as he grinned appreciatively at her toned legs.

"Peaches, I need to keep my distance or I'll be wearing cowboy boots, talking with a twang, and hitchhiking my way to Georgia in a week."

Kitty laughed and Jaycee's eyes slid to her friend, giving her a long, worried look.

***

Dash was dreaming. It was scorching hot down at the lake. He was on a boat, and no matter how many times he tried to dive into the water, he never made it. He kept finding himself back in the boat. It suddenly started to rain, but even that didn't cause the heat to ease. He heard Casper from a distance, her cries loud and plaintive and he struggled from the dream to see what was wrong. He felt rough hands grab him and he cried out. Unbearable pain seized him awake. Before blackness descended again, he smelled it. Thick acrid smoke.

***

The loud, rhythmic music exhilarated Jaycee. She danced to every song, not even knowing most of them. When her feet couldn't take anymore, she slipped out of the heels and hung them from her index finger as she danced.

It was she and John most of the night on the dance floor. He would ease nearer as he danced and then disappear into the crowd, only to appear closer than before and grabbing her waist to speak loudly into her ear over the music. Jaycee felt wary and confused...and flattered. He was attractive and seemed sweet enough, although a bit cocky.

Kitty would flit close as well and then Jaycee would see her across the room or dance floor, talking and laughing with friends. By three o'clock, they were exiting their fourth club and heading for breakfast a few blocks away.

"Ok," Jaycee said to Kitty as they walked the still-busy sidewalks of New York, buildings still holding them and the heat from the day captive. *The city that never sleeps.* She continued, "So you're *not* a morning person, you just hadn't gone to bed yet."

"Pretty much," Kitty said laughing. "You never asked."

"Um, when do you sleep?"

"Eight to noon."

"And work?"

"Monday through Thursday we keep tame hours. Home to bed by one."

Jaycee gulped. That would cut *three hours* off her nightly sleep.

John came up between the two of them, putting his arms around their waists as they walked. They arrived at the restaurant and he held the door for them. His penetrating gaze caught Jaycee's and his desire was clear. In her mind, she saw dark green eyes, not blue ones, and the particular tilt of another head. *Dash.*

She let her eyes wander to John's lips, wondering if it would be different to be kissed by him and not Dash. It felt wrong even to wonder, and she ducked her head, avoiding his gaze the rest of breakfast.

***

In a city of millions, how could she feel lonely? But the ache was still there. No matter the admiration, the expanse, the "things", she couldn't shake it. And sure, the city was fun; more distracting than Twain, but she realized....it didn't matter where she was, she couldn't run away from herself.

She slept fitfully and woke up several hours later to her phone ringing. Only one person called her phone and didn't text; her father.

She popped up off the inflatable mattress on Kitty's floor and answered the phone by the third ring.

"Hello?"

"Jaycee, it's Daddy."

"I thought so. Everything okay? Didn't Momma tell you I called when I arrived yesterday?"

"She did. We're glad you got there safely. I-I thought I should call – "

Hearing the worry in his voice, she asked, "What's happened? Is it Marcus or Momma?" Her heart began to race as a long pause met her question.

"No, they're fine. It's Dash. There's...there's been a fire."

Her legs crumpled then. She fell right where she stood, next to Kitty's dresser and onto the carpeted floor. Taking a deep breath, she found her voice and, working over the lump in her throat, she croaked out, "Tell me he's okay, Daddy."

Jaycee saw Kitty raise her head from her pillow. Time seemed to hesitate and Jaycee prayed silently, willing her father to reassure her.

"He's in ICU, unconscious and on a breathing machine. He's badly burned, but he's alive....."

His voice trailed off, leaving the last words unsaid, *For now.* Jaycee heard them echo and bounce around her chest, sinking deep into her heart. She bent over, touching her face to the carpet. Kitty came to her side and taking the phone from her hand, spoke quietly to Jaycee's father.

She didn't hear, *couldn't* hear. Life had stilled. *Fragile. Dash. Dash may not survive.* And in that moment, she didn't know if she could survive without him.

CHAPTER SEVEN

Kitty held her hand on and off, pulling Jaycee back to the present time and again on the train heading home. She had a strange feeling of being between two worlds; reality and her thoughts. Having completely fallen apart in Kitty's arms after she hung up the phone, she had become calm and resolute...determined to get home as quickly as possible.

The people, noise, and buildings that afternoon on the way to the train station were all obstacles between her and Dash.

What did I tell him? That she'd come if he needed her. He needed her. She needed him. He couldn't go and die, not now...not yet. Jaycee prayed more than any time in her childish, selfish, narrow existence of a life, not for her wants but for Dash's needs. To breath, to live, to grow. To have a wife and family someday. She shook the thoughts from her head and got serious...with God.

Oh God in heaven, please preserve his life...and mine. I'm so sorry, God. Such a shallow life and heart. Just yearnin' to be filled but ignoring the one who could fill me. I knew, Oh you know I knew, Lord. Been to church since I was a babe. I wasn't ready, too busy chasin' the shiny that I ignored and forgot You along the way. Forgive me, Jesus. I want to come back. Heal my heart. Heal Dash. Help him come back to me.

***

Dash's aunt Katie was in the ICU waiting room. She explained to Jaycee and Kitty how the nurse had come in to tend to Dash's burns a while ago, commenting that in a way his unconscious state was a blessing so he couldn't feel the pain the procedure would cause.

"Your parents have been here," Katie held back tears, "For just hours with me. I'm so grateful. Dash and I, it's just us left of the family...your momma as is close as I have besides him."

Jaycee's heart broke as she thought of the death of Dash's parents a few years ago. She sat next to Katie, holding her hand tightly.

"They won't let us in? Family only?" she questioned.

"You're his family as much as me; the amount of talk that boy has spent on Julia Cozetta Hamilton."

Jaycee gave a quiet, short laugh, which bounced off the sterile waiting room walls. "We've only been out a few times," she said aloud, remembering it really only being one time, except for their push-and-pull friendship over the years.

"My...he's talked incessantly about your over the years. Your braces coming off, and how you had to bring Jello to school to eat for a week. And that time you got stuck in the rain when your bike chain fell off and he gave you his jacket and wheeled it home for you." She looked at Jaycee. "I hope I'm not spilling the beans, but it's been a lifetime of Jaycee stories. I've come to know his love for you."

Jaycee wondered if he had told her the selfish parts. When she had yelled at him for that broken chain and him not being able to fix it or for the car overheating....and numerous other things over the years.

"I-I need him to be okay. There's so much I need to make up for, to apologize for."

"My dear, you have filled Dash's head with stars and wonder and as he got older, dreams of something that could be. I can't rightly say as he would know what you're apologizing for."

***

Jaycee and Katie took turns at Dash's bedside all week, occasionally taking a break to wash up, stretch, or change into clothes that Jaycee's mother brought.

The perpetual inflating and deflating of air in the bed to insure no bedsores lulled Jaycee with its constancy. She pulled her chair closer to him and reached for his hand, comforting in its warmth. She rubbed it gently and tucked her hand into his.

"Well, aren't you a sight. And here I thought we'd be goin' to the alumni football game together." She leaned closer to whisper near his ear, "I miss you." Tears stung her eyes as she looked at his expressionless face, grateful as she was that his color had improved over the course of the week.

He had been taken off the breathing tube the day before and was breathing evenly on his own with an oxygen mask. Part of his right arm and leg had been badly burned. The surgeons had harvested skin from his other leg and grafted this onto the burned areas. It would be a painful recovery, but he seemed to be improving slowly.

He groaned as if he had heard her, but remained expressionless. *Poor man is in some kind of pain.*

"I'm here. You rest now. I'm not goin' *anywhere.*" She stole a glance behind her at the drawn curtain and leaned over him, giving his cheek a quick kiss.

His eyes opened then, with her face so close to his. He looked aware and a twinkle caught in his eye at seeing her so near. She reached a hand up and stroked his cheek, the other still in his now strong clasp on the bed.

"You'll have to catch me for the next one, Dash Matheson. I'm countin' on a good chase, you hear?"

FALL

CHAPTER ONE

"One more play!" The tall quarterback yelled from the center of the field. The clock was winding down on the last quarter and the Twain High School alumni team was ahead by seven points over the Cooper High team.

Jaycee leaned over Dash in the stands, looking into his face. He had insisted they come. It was the first game since they'd graduated that he had missed playing in. He seemed to be taking it okay.

She rubbed her hands together and sat back on the bleachers. The metal seat was hard and getting colder as night fell. Her back ached. She stretched, loudly yawning as she did. Dash glanced her way and gave her a sheepish grin. "Tired?"

"I'll survive. You?"

"I've almost forgotten the pain." He added quietly, "It's been great. Thanks for humoring me."

"I'm just glad we came....together. And seein' you workin' those crutches certainly gave my heart pause." She winked at him and he grabbed her hand between his warm one and pulled her towards him.

"Come sit with me."

"I *am* sittin' with you."

"You know what I mean, closer."

Jaycee plastered her thigh next to his, feeling his warmth through the fabric of his pants. "I guess I shoulda' worn pants."

"Um, ya think?" He laughed now, glancing down at her jeans skirt and fashionable Ugg boots. A cheer came up from the crowd, pulling his attention back to the field. He put an arm across Jaycee's shoulders and hugged her to him.

***

"I am not goin', Jaycee," Dash said more sternly now.

Jaycee worried her lip between her teeth as she swiftly set the table, hearing the oven timer ring behind her in the tiny kitchen.

"But I need a wing man," she argued. She heard him sigh heavily before she turned back to the kitchen to retrieve dinner.

"Mmm, eggplant parm. Smells delicious," he called to her.

Upon reentering the room, she placed the hot casserole dish on the trivet and saw him quickly move his hand from his thigh and begin to stand.

"Sit." She spoke quietly as she crossed the small room to his side. "Is it aching tonight?"

He nodded, the pain evident in his eyes as she drew closer. Her phone beeped then, indicating a text message. She slid it from her pocket and hit silence, then put it on the coffee table upside down.

"Here," she instructed, "put yer leg across my lap." Jacyee sat and wiggled herself into a comfortable position.

"But the dinner."

"It needs to rest at least ten minutes."

He gave a wince, then relaxed as she gently worked the knotted flesh, careful not to touch the healing, tender skin.

"What would you do without me," she joked, smiling into his eyes across the couch.

"Um, not go to the Black Friday sales over in Lincoln next week."

"Ha-ha. Best sales of the year and you're gonna deny me?"

"You do what you will, darlin'. I've got no claim to deny you, but don't badger me to be part of your madness."

She stopped rubbing his leg for a moment and grabbed his hand. He laced his fingers through hers and puckered his lips. Jaycee leaned over, giving him a lingering kiss. Casper, Dash's cat, chose that moment to jump up on the back of the couch, nuzzling her head between the two of them. They both laughed.

"Not mad at me?"

"No," she sighed dramatically. "I was just hopin' you'd come charm the older women with those gallant manners so I could get some things first. Earliest sale starts at four am."

His gaze flew heavenward.

"And rollin' those pretty eyes won't get you free either. You may as well succumb to my charms."

"I already have," he laughed, "years ago." He wiggled his eyebrows at her now, suggestively.

"And no actin' that way around Momma and Daddy on Thanksgiving. They already have ideas about what I do hanging over here with you in this apartment."

His gaze grew serious, "They don't trust us?"

"Trust is one thing. Momma says hormones are another."

"Speaking of hormones, how has your new boss been behaving?" Dash's voice hardened as he asked the question.

She felt his thigh tense up again and she traced small circles on his leg with her free hand. Truth was, she didn't know how to deal with the issue.

"It's fine, Dash. I shouldn't have mentioned it. I need the job."

She'd been praying on how to handle Mr. Carlisle's over-friendly overtures. *Maybe it's my imagination.* But she felt uncomfortable around him.

"I don't trust him, Jaycee. He acted strange when I drove into Lincoln and took you to lunch last week."

"He's ancient, Daddy's age. They knew each other in high school." *What could happen?*

***

Dash cast his line into the water, listening
for the satisfying plop of the lure in the distance.
He glanced sideways at Jaycee as she wrangled the
crawler between two fingers and laced it on the
hook. She didn't wince or anything and for that, he
was mighty impressed.

She caught his gaze on her and smiled lazily,
"Told ya' I had fished before."

"True, just wasn't aware you could bait your
own hook."

She cocked an eyebrow in his direction and
turned her attention back to her reel, tightening
the line before casting. "My Daddy didn't raise no
squealers."

Dash laughed and watched as she made a
perfect cast by a spit of land that jutted into the
river. She leaned back against a nearby river birch.
He drew closer and adjusted the rod in his hand.
He put his arm briefly across her shoulder and

squeezed her firmly to him. "Now I can be sure I won't get hooked."

"Is that why you were standin' clear over t'other bank?"

"You know it."

Her giggle filled the cool fall air and hung about them, catching on the turning yellow leaves of the tree above them. She breathed in deeply and moved closer to Dash, kissing his cheek gently. "I'm so glad you invited me."

"Just wait," he said mischievously. "Hold my rod for a sec?"

She nodded to his question and he walked back to the truck, leaning on his cane, returning a few minutes later with a blanket and a cloth grocery bag. He spread the blanket quickly on the ground, casting a quick glance to the rods in Jaycee's hands for signs of movement. She arched her eyebrows and gave him a grin, "It's under control. What did ya' bring me to eat?"

Dash pulled a thermos and two travel mugs from the bag, along with chocolate éclairs in a clear plastic bakery box.

"Mmmm, you spoil me."

"Just enough."

They settled onto the blanket. Dash took his rod back and sat for a few minutes listening to the quiet of the day. The river gently lapped at the muddy bank and the loud call of a nearby northern bobwhite quail echoed over the other birds in the area.

He glanced at Jaycee in her yellow sweater set, jeans, and brown cowboy boots. "You warm enough," he worried, the sky being overcast and gloomy. Rain was expected, but he was hoping it would hold off until later in the day.

"Yes, thanks." She nodded and reached a hand for the thermos. "You want some?"

"You like hot spiced cider?"

"Oooo, yes." She poured them each some in the mugs and secured the lids, her fishing pole balanced in between her upright knees.

"Momma always made Daddy and I hot cider for our fishing trip the weekend before Thanksgiving." Dash swallowed over the sudden catch in his throat. He'd been coming here alone for the few years since his their deaths. Couldn't ruin tradition. But now, now he had someone to share it with again.

And what a woman. He still couldn't believe they were dating...a couple! His mind raced back to second grade on the playground at school. They had been playing Red Rover; the memory vivid because it was marred with the image of Jaycee with blood streaming down her chin. She had gotten her two front teeth knocked. Boy, she had given Stu Parkinson what for after he had run headlong into her and not into the clasped hands of the human chain as the game was supposed to be played. She had picked up her two front teeth

96

from the pavement at her feet and stomped off to the nurse's office. The boys were full of admiration and the girls present looked decidedly green.

She was determined then and to this day, that determination had driven Jaycee to be the best she could at whatever she put her mind to. He looked at her beautiful smile now. She was looking at him with a lightness in her eyes. Jutting her chin out, she looked at the éclairs. "You goin' to feed me one?"

"You trust me?"

"Yes." She looked at him then, askance, realizing his intent. "You best not squish that in my face, Dash."

"I'm reservin' that pleasure."

He could see her rolling that over in her mind. If she was standing, he swore she would have stomped that little boot clad foot of hers.

"No future talk. I'm still befuddled about what I want to be when I grow up," she said wryly.

"Well, one thing is fer sure. You need to quit workin' for Bruce Carlisle." He let it slip. He didn't mean to. He didn't want to ruin the day. This being a continual argument these past few weeks.

"It's good experience. I can handle him."

"But you shouldn't *have* to handle him. *That's* my point."

She was quiet then and he regretted bringing it up. He grabbed a disinfectant wipe from the bag and wiped his hands, offering her one which she accepted gratefully. He tried to lighten the mood again by reaching into the plastic box and lifting out the éclair. He wiggled it as he drew it closer to her mouth. She took a bite and chewed with relish.

He bit the other end and put it back into the box. His attention was caught by Jaycee's rod as her line tugged, the tip dipping deeply towards the ground.

"Looks like fish for dinner," he said smiling.

"You scale, I'll cook." Jaycee said, standing now and giving the line slack in increments as she reeled the fish in.

Just what his mother used to say to his Dad. A new tradition now. Their tradition.

"I wouldn't have it any other way."

***

"So?" Kitty asked without glancing up, engrossed with her phone.

"So, what?" Jaycee reiterated, blowing a chunk of long bangs out from in front of her eyes.

Lunch hadn't arrived yet and Kitty had been interacting more with someone by text than with Jaycee. She'd been trying to start a conversation for ten minutes now.

Jaycee grabbed her own phone from her bag, sliding her finger across the unlock feature.

Kitty lifted her head a moment later.

"Are you seriously texting me right now?"

"It seems the only way to get your attention," Jaycee said, covering her mouth with her hand as she laughed.

"Touché." Kitty put her head back down, but looked up with her eyes. "Darn technology. Makes you feel like you've lost your right arm if you're not on it constantly."

"Yeah, I guess." Now that Jaycee answered phones and worked on a computer most days, she found herself less inclined to reach for a gadget in her off hours.

Kitty, having put her phone away in her handbag, was all Jaycee's. "We're going to Aunt Myrtle's again."

"Nice. You love her stuffing." Jaycee said sarcastically, remembering how Kitty always complained about the strong spices in it. "We'll have it at home. I'm helpin' cook."

The look was classic Kitty. Her dark eyes opened incrementally until they looked huge in her small face. "You?"

"Yes, Daddy's not feeling so well. We're all pullin' more weight around the house and farm."

"I hope he's better soon."

"Thanks. He's been to the doctor. Had tests. We'll see." She sighed and looked around the small restaurant. Marlene didn't work until the afternoon shift and Karl's Diner was quiet. "Glad you could come home."

"Me too. Nothing like a mundane Twain, Georgia fall day to catch up on my rest." She yawned dramatically, letting one arm laze high above her right ear.

Jaycee eyed the circles under her friend's eyes. "Still livin' the party lifestyle?"

"It's like a whole other layer of marketing in the fashion magazine world. It's not an option; it's required. Be seen. Keep current. Know your stuff." She glanced down at her slate gray cashmere sweater and gave Jaycee a lopsided grin.

"That's alotta pressure. I didn't see that side, not stayin' for long."

"Yeah, that was a shame. Poor Dash," Kitty said, referencing to the house fire that he had gotten caught in. Taking her glass of Diet Coke with her, she sat back in the booth. "We could try again."

Jaycee laughed. "My speed's somewhere between tall buildings and shanties." Almost as an afterthought she added, "Besides. Dash is here."

"He is," Kitty said, and then added almost reluctantly, "Just don't settle."

Jaycee felt her face grow warm. "Stayin' here. He's just one piece. I don't know. Twain is just part of who I am."

Kitty shook her head. "I never thought it of you. And John? He's been texting you for months, right?"

"He's *your* roommate. We're just friends. He likes to hear about country life." Jaycee had guilt over this one. Dash had wondered at the texts and seen John's name on more than one occasion. *Just a friend*. Nothing deceitful there.

"And Dash?"

"He knows what he wants. He's not lookin' to peddle himself to anyone, including me. He's just…Dash."

"And you're just Jaycee. You're not married, you know."

"I've been prayin' on it, what I should be doin'."

"For real?" Kitty asked skeptically.

"All that stuff in Sunday school, youth, church….it's makin' more sense now. I-I think God will direct my steps. I'm just waitin' on *Him*….not Dash."

The food arrived on the tail of her sentence. Jaycee eyed her blue cheese bacon burger, thinking of running half to Dash on her way back home. "I just wish He'd hurry up. Can't rush God, though."

"Something else going on?"

Jaycee grabbed the ketchup and made a puddle on her plate. "My boss. I've been callin' him Mister Creeper. He makes me uncomfortable."

"Got Raid?"

"What?" Jaycee asked, looking up with interest.

"We girls keep a can on our desks or in a drawer for such a time as needed. Lotsa Mister Creepers in the world."

"But – what do I *do*?"

"Jaycee Cozetta Hamilton, you know what to do if he gets outta line."

"But he's Daddy's friend."

"Blood's thicker than water and your Daddy'd be the first one to deck him."

Jaycee considered for a moment and nodded. "Truer words."

CHAPTER TWO

The Monday through Friday grind didn't loom so large this week as Jaycee entered the small hallway on the ground floor of the office complex. Thanksgiving was only four short days away. A large sign on the door signified Carlisle Realty.

She tried the door only to find it locked and leaned against the wall next to it. Shifting her handbag off her shoulder, she reached for her phone. Before she had it pulled out, Eleanor appeared from the parking lot entrance.

"Sorry, I'm late."

"Only minutes. No worries."

Jaycee entered the three room office behind Eleanor as she flipped on the light and adjusted the thermostat. Her desk was as she had left it. She adjusted her chair and leaned over to push the power button on the computer tower. She heard Eleanor do the same at her desk.

"How was yer weekend?"

"Nice," Jaycee answered. "Caught a few fish with Dash. That was the highlight."

"The fish or Dash?"

"Well...Dash," Jaycee said grinning at her across the expanse of their two desks. "And your weekend?"

"Great. Moved the last of the boxes to the new place."

"So you're really leavin' me?" Jaycee frowned now. Eleanor had trained her for the position and Jaycee had only been there a few short months.

"'Fraid so." Eleanor looked at her sympathetically. "I'm sure he'll hire another girl soon."

Jaycee nodded her head. Her mind refused to accept she'd be alone in the office with *The Creeper*. She suddenly remembered the can of Raid in her purse and slid it out, placing it against the desk leg.

"You know, you don't have to stay. I –
maybe I should have warned you."

This was the nearest either of them had
gotten to talking about their boss' advances. Jaycee
looked up hopefully at Eleanor. "You've been here
how long?"

"A year. We don't last long." Eleanor
heaved a loud sigh.

Jaycee looked around to see if Mr. Carlisle
was in the room then whispered, "Why doesn't
someone report him? This can't keep happenin'."
She raised her voice then, getting angrier as she
spoke. "Land sakes, I don't want to train a girl for
this."

Eleanor pursed her pouty red lips. Tossing
her ebony hair over her shoulder, she shrugged.
"No time to make trouble. Everyone's strugglin'.
We gotta work."

"Yeah, but not like this!"

"So quit. You live at home. You don't need
the money like some girls."

"He's my daddy's friend."

Eleanor nodded slowly. "I get it. Find somethin' else quick."

"No," Jaycee said determinedly. "I think I'll be rectifyin' the situation."

"How are you going do that?"

"Not sure yet, but harvest time's comin'."

Eleanor grinned suddenly and slapped her desk. "Wish I could stick around for that!"

***

Dash kicked the counter before him in frustration. The pain vibrated from his steel toe boot and up his thigh. *Good thing that was my good leg.*

He was sick of paperwork, calling suppliers, finding parts, and getting stuck in the front office. He wanted to be working on cars, not be a secretary. He and Chuck used to both make the calls and do the paperwork. Now the bulk of the car fixing fell to Chuck, and Dash was stuck in customer service. Not that he minded the interaction with the townsfolk; he just wanted to get his hands dirty again.

He looked down at the wooden cane leaning against the counter. Jaycee's dad had given it to him, something to work towards when he left the hospital. From wheelchair to crutches to this. Slow and steady progress. It just wasn't fast enough. He needed to increase volume, advertise, but with only one mechanic things had stalled out. His savings was slowly dwindling, between paying the utilities on the shop, Chuck's salary, and rent on the apartment. He certainly couldn't foresee forward movement with Jaycee when he was in this state.

Mercy, God. How much more pain, loss? Will I lose Jaycee too?

Dash had seen the texts. Jaycee's furtive glances at them. He had even asked who John was. Someone she had met briefly in New York. Was she going to go back to him? Was there more to *just friends* than even Jaycee was aware of, deep down?

* * *

Mr. Carlisle had been out with clients all morning, but was back in his office now with the door closed. Jaycee typed the last of the new listings in and uploaded them to MLS. Fiddling with her pen and seeing Eleanor on a call, she pulled out a piece of copy paper to make the start of a tentative grocery list.

Daddy not feeling well had left them all wondering how Thanksgiving would go. Jaycee was gone weekdays and quite a bit of his chores had fallen onto her mother and to Marcus after school. Jaycee was determined to take up some of the slack in the evenings when she returned home and to help with Thanksgiving shopping and food prep.

Turkey. Cranberries. Flour. Brown sugar.
Potatoes. Cornmeal. Green beans.

Jaycee went down the list, adding
ingredients to dishes, leaving plenty of space at the
bottom for her mother to write in additional items.
She realized as she ticked down dishes in her head,
she had forgotten to tell Dash she would be scarce
this week. She had told him briefly Daddy had gone
for tests last week, but hadn't gone into detail, not
wanting to ruin the special Thanksgiving fishing trip
that past Saturday.

Eleanor gave a loud sigh as she hung up the
phone. "Gotta leave early today. Ok'd it with the
boss." She tidied her desk top and moved toward
the break room with her coffee cup in hand. "I'll
make a fresh pot before I leave," she called back to
Jaycee.

Jaycee nodded, though she realized Eleanor
couldn't see her. One thing she had learned first
was to keep the coffee pot full of fresh coffee all

day long. Probably why Mr. Carlisle was so hyper and couldn't sit still.

Eleanor left a short time later with a backward wave.

Jaycee glanced at her boss' closed door. It wasn't often she was alone with him. He had cornered her briefly in the break room when she was eating her lunch several times. Since then, she had eaten in her car or at a nearby delicatessen, Sandwich on the Sly.

She answered several calls and finished her list, slipping the paper into her purse. Her foot kicked the can of Raid several times as the day wore on and each time, a feeling of trepidation clutched at her heart. *What am I so worried about anyway?* Jaycee could outrun him and she had a mean right hook on the outside chance she couldn't. *How dare he make me feel so out of control and vulnerable!*

It was 4:30 when Jaycee saw his office door swing open. She was on the phone scheduling an appointment for him to view a house with a buyer for the next day.

"This coffee fresh?" She heard him question from the back room.

"Yes." *God, forgive me for the lie. I cannot go in that little room with him.* What would she do when the week was over? Eleanor would be gone. "You want me to place an ad in the Dollar Saver?"

Mr. Carlisle rounded the corner. His brown eyes fell on Jaycee and then cast their way towards Eleanor's empty desk. He stepped closer to Jaycee's desk, the computer monitor between them.

Jaycee comforted herself by banging the toe of her high heel shoe against the tin can at her feet, making a slight echoing sound in the room.

"What's that," he questioned Jaycee on the sound.

"Bug spray." She said, raising her chin and meeting his eyes. "For bugs."

Mr. Carlisle squinted at her then, lifting the coffee cup to his lips. "So an ad? Already?"

"Eleanor's last day is Wednesday."

"We could see how things go...you and me holding down the fort."

The phone rang then, interrupting the retort on Jaycee's tongue. She lifted the phone. "Carlisle Realty. How can I help you?"

"Hello, darlin'."

Dash's smooth deep voice melted some of Jaycee's taut nerves. She put a finger up to Mr. Carlisle, who had settled his trim 50-something figure atop the front of her desk.

"Well, hi there, Dash. What can I do for you?" Her voice sounded strange, even to her own ears. She took a few shallow breaths and averted her eyes from her boss to the computer screen.

Dash's tone lost some of its playfulness. "Um, things okay, Jaycee?"

"Yes. Just finishin' up for the day. I won't be by, forgot to tell you. Gotta finish the grocery list with Momma tonight for Thursday."

"Sure enough. Listen, call me when you get a chance later. I wanted to ask you somethin'."

"I will. I'll talk to you then."

"Okay. Bye. And remember....you need me, you call."

"Bye." Jaycee hung up the phone. Mr. Carlisle hadn't moved a muscle since the phone had rung, which was unlike him in all respects.

"How's that Daddy of yours doing anyways?"

"Just fine, thank you." She'd be darned if she'd discuss her Daddy with him, even if they were old friends.

"I don't happen to have plans on Thanksgiving. Think I could get a good meal? If I remember right, your Momma sure knows how to cook."

Jaycee squirmed in her seat, avoiding eye contact with the man. She swore she saw him try to peek down her blouse as she busied her hands with paperwork.

She contemplated a moment longer than was proper. "I'll check with my folks." She squeezed out.

"Right nice. Much needed sustenance to these old bachelor bones." He flexed his arm as if on display, then gathered his now dry coffee cup. "You can go now. We'll talk tomorrow."

She nodded and made quick order of turning off her computer and stacking several files in her inbox. When he had turned and was half-way to his office, she grabbed the bug spray, slipped it into her purse, and escaped out the door.

CHAPTER THREE

"Follow-ups tomorrow," her mother said, as she and Jaycee sat at the kitchen table with her mother's recipe book open between them.

"All those tests. Glad maybe we'll have some answers." Jaycee smiled encouragingly then and laughed, trying to reassure her momma. "I hope they can fix him."

Her mother's quiet laugh joined Jaycee's. "Maybe not the orneriness, but the shakes and tremors would be nice." They sobered not long after, her mother's eyes clouding. "Such a time to be sick, with the holidays comin'."

"We'll manage. Clyde's been handlin' the cattle. We got the chickens and horses all set. Marcus is a pro. I manage." Jaycee grimaced.

"You never were one for dirt, manure, or farm smells, my dear."

"I'll do the bulk of the cookin', Momma. I know you're tired after bein' outside."

"We'll have to hire another hand soon, though your daddy is stubbornly against it. My feet and back are just sheer wore out by the end of the day. I can supervise, chop and stir sittin' down, though. "

"And pester, badger, and tell me what I'm doin' wrong."

"Now, Jaycee."

"I'm just kiddin'. I'm happy to help. I love to cook, just like you."

"I didn't know that." Her mother flipped the pages in the book, tapping her finger on the recipe before them. "We must make this too."

"Um, yeah...like 12 of them." She giggled. It was a family favorite.

"You're makin' them. You wanna make 12?"

Jaycee looked at the recipe for her mother's pecan pie. "No, but I'll make three. We have enough pecans stored up?"

"Yes, there are a few bags left."

"How about a pumpkin and an apple?"

Her mother nodded, "That should be good."

Jaycee nodded. "That reminds me. Mr. Carlisle has nowhere to go. Okay for me to invite him?" *Creepy freeloader.*

Her momma didn't look up at that. A moment passed then she responded, her eyes still on the list before her. "Yes, he can come. We'll have plenty. The Lord has been good to us. We must bless others with what we have been blessed with."

The doorbell rang then. Marcus yelled Jaycee's name from the front hall. As she walked from the kitchen, worry pulled her through the living room to check on her father. He was asleep in his favorite chair before the television. She pulled a quilt from the couch and placed it across his legs, tiptoeing from the room.

She waggled her eyebrows at Marcus as he stood talking to Dash and put her finger to her lips.

"Daddy's sleepin'. Gol'durn, you could wake the dead."

***

Dash had been stewing all day; so much so, he reckoned he could make his own gravy. Marlene had given him a sympathetic shake of her head as she plopped his fried steak and gravy before him. He chewed it absently and greeted Tucker Meltzer and his new wife, Cora Leigh, then downed his second glass of pop. Without much forethought to the consequences, he went barreling over the Jaycee's house not long after the supper crowd had cleared from the diner.

Jaycee scolding her younger brother should have warned him off to the sort of mood she was in. He followed her slowly, leaning on his cane, as she led him silently back outside and around the house and to the porch, opening the screen door for him to enter.

"I told ya' I'd be busy tonight, Dash." Jaycee sat in a cushioned wicker chair. "Thanksgiving is almost here and Momma and I are in a rush for sure to get things set right."

He pulled a chair closer to her side and pushed his long legs straight out in front of him as he sat. "I can't seem to escape my worryin'. I'm sorry to show up without callin'."

"What're you rollin' yer mind over?" She turned in her chair to face him, hitching a bare foot up to rest on the cushion. Absently she twirled a strand of her short blonde hair over her index finger.

"You and me. Your job." He met her gaze and gulped, wanting to take her in his arms and kiss her sweet mouth, to make reason and thinking and working out the pieces of life flee. "I should clarify, your *boss*."

"Land sakes, what does my boss have to do with you and me?" She dropped her hand and huffed out a breath of air so loud it scattered the piece of hair she had been twisting.

"I'm afraid for ya' with that randy man sniffin' around you day after day. Can't get no peace over it. And....and." He paused. Maybe it wasn't a good idea to go further tonight with this.

"And?" Jaycee stiffened in her chair, her eyes growing wide.

"And you and that John texting all the time. I may be a gimp, but I'm not blind or stupid, Jaycee."

"Are you accusin' me of somethin', Dash Matheson?" She was on her feet now with her face red and two fists on her hips. Her mouth worked to say more and he could tell she was trying to remember the Southern manners her momma had taught her.

"Don't you be gettin' all holier than thou, Julia Cozetta. I've known you since we were nappin' in Ms. Carter's kindergarten class. You've been hidin' some things and it's time we get them out in the open."

"I cannot do this now. I just cannot!" Jaycee fled to the front of the house then, leaving the screen door to slam in multiple successions in her wake.

He hadn't moved. He was planted there. He put his hand to his thigh and rubbed it absently before he went to stand, grasping the hard cane in his right hand. He wanted to wing it through the screen and out across the fields that stretched behind the house and barn. But he needed it, to get by…just like he needed Jaycee. And he didn't know if he could discard her so easily either. But she had to make up her mind. No more dallying with a fantasy of a man. He was flesh and blood. He saw her quiet smile sometimes when she glanced at her phone, thinking he didn't see. It was time to throw caution to the wind and see where things landed on the other side of reason.

***

The audacity of the man was too much. Jaycee thought of John only as a friend. The cryptic words flashed through her mind then. Innuendo-laced messages had passed back and forth. She pulled at the loose thread on her comforter, yanking harder than she had intended, a hole opening up at the seam.

Men! Always with their feathers rufflin' about somethin' and struttin' around puffed up because of the littlest flirtation. Was this what John was, a flirtation? Or a possibility kept waiting in the wings? He made her feel exciting and admired. But didn't Dash do that? No, he was steadfast and so not full of....empty compliments. It was as if Jaycee could see each and every message for what it was. That's all that John gave her, a head full of herself. They had only met once and it was a nanosecond compared to the course of memories with Dash...since grade school.

Jaycee suddenly felt ashamed of herself. A pit in her stomach opened up a mile wide and crept up to her chest, causing an ache in her heart. Her phone vibrated for the second time in ten minutes and without looking, she threw it against her bedroom door where it fell and shattered into pieces on the floor.

***

It was a long day, made even longer still with no form of communication with the outside world. It was a bad habit, Jaycee was aware of that; having her phone on the desk in front of her while working. It was for the best, for now, no phone. She needed to clear her mind and this was the best way. No distractions. Just work-related calls and duties.

She'd been praying all morning about her father's appointment at the doctor's and about Dash. She wondered if he had tried to call or text her. Well, he knew the number at the office sure enough.

She reminded Eleanor she was leaving early and at half-past three, Jaycee patted the grocery list in her purse tucked next to her mother's debit card as she made her way to the parking lot.

The afternoon was cloudy and overcast with the wind increasing since the morning. Mr. Carlisle had just pulled into his spot when she appeared from the building. Jaycee made her way quickly across to where she was parked. She wasn't quick enough, for he bounded from his car and over to where she stood attempting to unlock the door of her Chrysler Lebaron.

"Where you off to?" he asked from behind her as she fumbled with the key. She slowly inclined her head towards him. He positioned his body against the side of her car and faced her boldly.

"I told you I had to leave early today, helpin' momma shop for Thursday."

"Ahh, so you can feed me well, yes?" He reached out and touched her arm, running his hand down the length of it and ending at her hand.

Jaycee pulled her hand away and stuck it into her purse underneath her other arm, where she left it. "Th-that's right, sir."

"How about we go for an early dinner? You know what they say about shopping on an empty stomach." He stepped nearer, closing the short distance between them. He smiled, looking down at her lips and licking his own.

She backed away, which left her further from escape into her car. "I'm not hungry." Her stomach twisted in knots as he again stepped closer. Woods bordered the parking lot and she felt the ground give underneath her foot as she crossed from the pavement and into the dirt. "It would seem *you* are though."

He smirked. "So you can tell my desire for you, my southern flower."

"I'm not your anything." Heat flooded Jaycee's face. She couldn't run. *She wouldn't*. She stood her ground then, not moving towards the seeming safety of the woods or back to the parking lot. "Don't come any closer." She grasped the cold metal between her fingers and pulled it from her purse. She turned the can around and aimed it at him.

"Is this a joke?" He laughed, but it held a higher pitch than normal.

"No joke. Is *this* a joke, all this?" She raised her other hand indicating where she was in relation to her car. "I am done. I will *not* take it anymore."

"Take what? We were just having a conversation."

"Dinner? Southern flower?" She shook the can at him, frustrated with his conceit.

He didn't back away. He looked like he was pondering his next move. He glanced down at his feet and back up again, shuffling slightly forward. Jaycee exploded with her next words, nearly shouting them, straightening the arm holding the can. "You aren't temptin' me, are you?"

"Am I tempting you?" He smiled smoothly.

"To put you down like a bug, that's about it." Jaycee saw movement behind Mr. Carlisle and heard her name. He heard as well, because he turned at the sound, backing up a step.

"That's right, you should back off." Dash stood there, his face a cloud of fury. He drew closer and grabbed the side of Mr. Carlisle's shirt, tossing him towards the parking lot and advancing after him.

"Dash!" Jaycee called, dropping the can of Raid on the ground and chasing after the two of them.

"Enough, Jaycee. I'm not stupid and either is he. The leering, suggestions, and now this, practically accosting you and chasing you into the woods."

She stopped in her tracks. He stood there between her and Mr. Carlisle. His breath was coming in short gasps as he struggled to gain control of his temper.

"I know." She shook her head, fighting the tears as they came into her eyes and fell to her cheeks. She could see his indecision. They had to talk, she knew it. He knew it. The pain on his face was very real.

And then there was Mr. Carlisle, backed up against his car, glancing towards the office building, gauging the distance to his escape. Jaycee walked towards the man, not getting any closer than Dash himself, standing by his side.

"I quit. I won't work for you anymore. *You will be reported.* Whether it does any good, well...that's up to the Better Business Bureau or whoever. You're not my problem anymore."

Mr. Carlisle's eyes narrowed at Jaycee. "But-but Eleanor's leaving. You can't –"

"I can." She faced Dash, feeling drained. With tears in her eyes, she tried to smile. "Thanks." With Dash's attention on her, Mr. Carlisle ran for the office building and was gone in less than a minute.

Jaycee turned towards her car, unlocked the door and slid into the seat. She couldn't apologize, she was numb. She slammed the car door between her and Dash. Her whole body was shaking. Anger, relief, frustration washed over Jaycee all at once. She stared into her lap, the keys grasped tightly between her fingers. When she finally looked up, he was gone. She knew he was still mad at her for John and her dishonesty....with him and herself. As she eased the car out onto the main road towards Super Shopper, a gentle rain began to fall along with Jaycee's freely flowing tears.

CHAPTER FOUR

Dash drove his truck back from Lincoln to Twain, the silence in the cab mocking him. Every few seconds he heard a ping though from the rebuilt 1950 engine. He shook his head and leaned forward, concentrating on the noise and breaking down the components in his mind, analyzing the sound and possible source.

He pulled into the shop's back parking lot and into the open bay door. Chuck was still working on replacing the struts in Kay McGrath's old Volvo. He waved to Dash from beside the car.

Dash nodded to him as he exited the still running vehicle, "Gotta look at her engine."

"You want me to do it?"

"Naw, I can. Any calls?"

"A few scheduled," Chuck said, casting a glance over to the cordless phone and appointment book.

"Thanks. Sorry to leave you short."

Chuck grunted, already back under with the Volvo. Dash took a rag from the workbench, shining a piece of chrome absently before pulling open the truck's hood. He stepped closer, listening intently to the whir of the engine. A quiet sigh escaped him. He put his head directly under the hood, concentrating. He didn't hear it.

He walked back around to sit behind the wheel. Holding his breath, he focused again. He didn't hear the sound. Slamming his hand on the steering wheel in frustration, he flipped the engine off and let out a flow of silent complaints up to heaven. His parent's car accident, the fire, everything but memories gone in a moment, and now a rift with Jaycee. He couldn't even seem to diagnose his own truck without a call for help.

Dash could feel Chuck's eyes on him and he poked his head out the open door. "Can't hear it. I'll leave it here and see if it does it again on the way home."

"Low test knocking?"

Dash shook his head as he slammed the driver's door and grabbed the phone and appointment book. He headed up the stairs and into the shop office, moving with a more pronounced limp from a weariness of the soul only prayer and seeking God could alleviate. *Almost Thanksgiving and all I can think about is what I don't have.* Plopping into the office chair behind the counter, he pulled open the bottom drawer and reached for his bible.

***

Jaycee's Momma, Daddy, and brother all gathered at the kitchen table. Several bags filled with groceries stood on the counter, the cold and frozen items shoved quickly away on Jaycee's return. This was the moment that had plagued her all day, that and thoughts of Dash and their fight.

Her mother looked at her daddy calmly and he nodded her into speech. "It would seem your daddy has the early stages of Parkinson's disease. All the studies were to rule out other things. The neurological exams point to it." She looked into the shocked eyes of Jaycee and Marcus. "It's going to be okay. *He's* going to be okay. They have medications now that will most likely help his symptoms at bay for years to come."

"What can we do?" Jaycee asked.

"Medication, for right now anyways. We'll see what works for him. It may take several weeks."

"What does that mean, Momma?" Marcus moved closer to her as he spoke. She pulled him the last few inches towards her and held him in her lap.

Jaycee was suddenly reminded that he was still only twelve; just a kid.

"It means we have an answer and should be grateful." The hand not holding Marcus on her lap was suddenly clasped by Jaycee's father from across the table.

"That's right. I'll be fine, in time. We need to give thanks it isn't something worse." His mouth trembled slightly as he spoke, but his words were strong.

Jaycee stood and went to his side, putting her hand on his shoulder. "We'll all do what we can 'til yer better." *Would he get better? This would be a lifelong fight.* She took a deep breath, not really planning on revealing her job situation until after Thanksgiving. "I'll be around to help more....during the day. I quit my job."

She saw everyone's head swing in her direction. "Now what did ya' go and do something dumb like that for," Marcus exclaimed, slipping from his mother's lap and back into his own chair. He pushed his chin into both hands, waiting for an explanation.

Her parents were silent, though her mother didn't look nearly as surprised as the rest of them.

"I guess you could say that Mr. Carlisle and I didn't get along."

"Meaning?" Her Daddy asked, his eyebrows lifting.

"Daddy, I know he's yer friend and I appreciate that him knowin' you when I applied might have helped get me the job."

Her father interrupted. "We were friends a long time ago, Pumpkin, not recently. Did he do something?"

Jaycee's momma moved from the table and went to stand by Jaycee who had shifted closer to the refrigerator, the cool steel at her back.

"Well, he was quite the showboat in his day. I suspect he still is. Is that the case?"

Jaycee nodded silently, tears stinging the insides of her eyelids.

"You did the only sensible thing then. We sure can use you 'round here for a spell anyhow. Right nice of God to work things out for us. He can use the bad for good, right, dear?" She asked this pointedly to Jaycee's father.

He stood then too, pushing his chair out and steadying himself momentarily with a hand on the table. "He surely can." He passed Marcus's chair and chucked him across the head, giving him a grin as he headed towards the living room. "It'll be nice havin' you both here more this week."

"I expect you're tuckered out from doctor's visit. I'll bring you in some coffee, pills, and your fried onions." Jaycee's momma turned and her gaze met Jaycee's own. She squished up her face at the mention of the offending food, but at the same time a smile curved her lips. They were both glad Daddy and his onions would be a part of their lives for a while to come.

***

Wednesday morning passed quickly for Jaycee. She took over the cleaning of the house from her Momma, who went out with Marcus to take care of the livestock. Her father slept in and she tiptoed on slippered feet through much of the chores.

The home phone was quiet, ominously so. She hadn't heard from Dash. What was he thinking? Was he still mad about John? She hadn't had a chance to tell him about her broken phone so, maybe he thought *she* was mad at *him.* Or...could be he thought she *chose* John over him.

Her heart dropped when the thought crossed her mind. She never was one to wax poetic about any man. Romantic movies on TV only further irritated her about how sappy love could be. It didn't stop her from having that certain yearning though, where Dash was concerned. He was a man, sure enough, and not just the annoying boy who had chased her since she was old enough to dress herself. She missed him with each fiber of her flesh and every heartbreakingly sorry threaded breath.

The back door slammed, pulling Jaycee from her funk. She had been leaning against a kitchen chair, fingering the recipes for the pies she need to start.

Her Momma came up beside her, pushing her phone into her hand. "It's Kitty." She walked back out the back door to give her privacy.

"Hello?" Jaycee said, putting the phone to her ear.

"Girl, what is going on with your phone? I have to call your Momma to get you?"

"It's busted." *No need to explain further*.

"John's been trying to get you and blowin' up my phone!"

"Seriously?"

"Well, sure. I'll text him your phone's DOA."

"I'm goin' to get another this afternoon, before everything closes down."

"How's your daddy?"

Jaycee's brain formed the word before she could push it through her throat. It came out as a croak and her eyes filled with tears as she uttered, "Parkinson's."

Silence and then Kitty's stricken voice, "Oh! I'm so sorry."

"Thanks. He'll be ok." Her strong, capable, generous Daddy...with Parkinson's. The shakes and tremors, the swaying as he tried to regain his balance. *Lord, heal him. I'm not ready to say goodbye yet.*

And suddenly, Jaycee remembered Dash...all alone. No Momma or Daddy. And she had disappeared as well, with no more than a flip of her corn silk hair, out of his life.

"I gotta go, Kitty. I'll text you when I get my new phone."

Jaycee hung up and immediately punched in Dash's number. It was picked up on the second ring.

"Hello?"

"Hi, Dash. It's me, Jaycee."

"Well, I was sorta wonderin' what your Momma would want with me." His voice warmed Jaycee's heart.

"My phone's broke. I realized I hadn't told you."

"I've been leavin' you to yer thoughts." A long pause followed his words. "Do you want to meet later when I get off work?"

"Yes, I'd like that." She found she had been holding her breath and let the air out in a long whoosh.

"My place then, seven-ish?" She could hear relief in his voice as he spoke.

"Sounds good. I'll finish the bakin' by then."

***

Three pecan, two pumpkin, and two apple pies covered the kitchen table cooling. Jaycee's Momma's double oven had helped the process go a lot smoother. Jaycee had even enlisted her father's help by having him shell the pecans. She had made quick order of the pumpkin mixture after making the pie crusts. Once those were in the oven, she had pared and cut the apples, adding the cinnamon, nutmeg, and sugars to the top of the heaping apples then turning them gently before piling the whole fall-smelling goodness into the pie tins. The pecan pies took a bit longer, but it was now with some satisfaction that Jaycee paused to survey the table before her.

While the last of the pies were in the oven earlier, Jaycee had pulled out one of her grandmother's crewel tablecloths to grace the long shiny mahogany table in the dining room. She stopped there briefly to add two burgundy candles in holders to the center. Glancing at the large clock on the buffet table, she noted the time and hurried to her room to change. Time to meet Dash!

It didn't take Jaycee long to change. She chose jeans and a burgundy sweater. She took an ivory scarf and twisted it around her neck artfully.

Grabbing her boots as she walked, she met her Momma in the kitchen where she sat down to yank them on.

"The pies look amazing, dear." Her mother stepped close to kiss her on the cheek.

"Thanks, Momma. Boy howdy, what a show that was."

"Troubles?"

"No, not at all. Just lots of balancing and timing."

"Yes, that is one of the secrets of making a Thanksgiving dinner, timing. And you've been so much help already!"

"I'm off to see Dash, maybe grab a phone on the way if the store's still open."

"That's fine. Gonna sit and prep some of the veggies tonight."

"And the turkey?"

"Goes in early morning. I'll take care of that and we'll do the rest together after."

Jaycee nodded, fully aware how much of this her momma had done all these years on her own. Sure Jaycee had done some chopping and stirring, but the bulk of the cooking had been her momma's responsibility.

"I love you, Momma. Thanks for all you do."

"And I love you, pumpkin. You're all worth it."

CHAPTER FIVE

It was past sunset. Streaks from the last rays of the sun caught on the clouds, like a woman's pink-tinged cloak. The bare trees on the roadside tangled in the wind, dark in contrast against the sky. A cold snap was in the forecast. Thanksgiving eve. And there he was, broken down on the way home.

The truck had started sputtering three minutes into the drive. He should have turned back to the shop, but he figured he could make it home. Less than ten minutes later, the truck engine had died completely. He stood beside the open hood, his hands jammed into his jeans pockets. He was too tired to be angry or frustrated. It was what it was and if he hadn't been so prideful earlier in the shop, Chuck could have diagnosed the minute sound he had heard, which had obviously been a larger issue.

Dash saw lights bounce against the trees and a car turned down the tiny side road. He shielded his eyes as it approached and pulled behind the truck on the shoulder of the road. The lights remained on, blinding him as he heard the driver's door open.

"I told ya', Dash," a breathy female voice said, mimicking his own from when he had rescued Jaycee that fateful hot July day month's earlier.

She walked in front of the headlights, her silhouette swaying slowly. She drew closer and he saw her gentle smile.

"My hero," he said, reaching through the glare and wrapping his arms around her as she stepped into his embrace.

"Oh, Dash. I've been such a fool."

"Have you now?" He felt a well-spring of joy spring up from his heart. He rested his chin atop her head "I hadn't noticed."

"The John thing, I – I should explain. It was stupid." She hesitated, but he was silent, waiting for her to go on. "You aren't makin' this easy on me, are ya?"

He shook his head, waiting. He didn't want to wonder at her actions anymore. He wanted to know and hold no doubts about her.

"It was dumb, the start of it and the continuation of something out of nothing. I – I met him in New York. He's Kitty's roommate." It was getting colder, the wind picking up, and as Jaycee floundered, Dash pulled her with him to lean against the bed of the truck. She tucked her head against his chest and continued. "I don't have feelin's for him, not even when I was there. I don't know why I let it continue. Please forgive me. I'll be tellin' him when I get the new phone set up."

"It's over, Jaycee?" He felt her nod against his chest. "Of yer own volition? I'm not forcin' you, ya know. I just need to be sure of where your....heart is." This stumbled from his mouth. It wasn't like him to ask for validation.

She stepped back from his arms. He saw her face clearly in the light from her car....which meant she saw his. He looked deeply into her eyes, the words screaming from his brain to his heart and back again. He wouldn't be the first to say it though. He couldn't. Not after...everything.

"I love you, Dash Matheson. There is no one I would rather be with in my whole life than you." She breathed the words softly and came close to his lips with her own, hovering near enough for him to feel her bated breath.

"And I love you, Julia Cozetta Hamilton." He leaned in, meeting her the rest of the way to claim her lips. Her hands flew to the back of his neck and pressed him closer, warming them both against the descending night.

***

Thanksgiving came early at the Hamilton household. Jaycee was up at daybreak to help

Marcus with the chickens and feeding the horses. Her steps were light across the frost covered ground. Humming as she worked, she put fresh water into the troughs.

Dash loved her! It was Thanksgiving and he was coming. Not long now, he would walk through their front door with his Aunt Katie. The flash in his eyes when he first glimpsed her and that tender look he gave her when they spoke, she knew what it all meant now. Love.

Not fascination or excitement for some imagined thing, but a desire of the heart to care for someone outside of yourself. She felt it. She knew now what love was. Over the months that they had dated, she hadn't wanted to put a name to it. And the conversations with John distracted her. Though weighing heavily on her conscience, they had kept her heart strings from being too attached. She now knew it was fruitless, to hold back or to deny what she truly felt.

She was in love with Dash Matheson. And she didn't know when it had started along the way, just that it had grown, budded, and now was in full bloom.

She slid her sneakers from her feet before entering the kitchen. The smell of turkey teased at Jaycee and her stomach growled loudly.

"Sit on down and warm up," Jaycee's Momma clucked around her. "My, your cheeks are red. Let me get you some coffee and monkey bread."

"Oooo, you made monkey bread!"

"Now don't you be silly, of course I did."

Jaycee grinned at her momma's back as she turned towards the coffee pot on the counter, eyeing the fluted Bundt pan full of gooey sugary bread. She rubbed her hands together to warm up then got up to wash them beneath hot sudsy water.

"The pies are in on the buffet. I decorated the table with a centerpiece your daddy had delivered late yesterday." Her momma fairly beamed at this declaration, sliding coffee and a plate full of food onto the table. "He's feelin' slightly better today, praise God!"

"Amen, Momma." Jaycee sat again, taking a long sip of the hot elixir. "And Happy Thanksgiving." She stood again and walked over to where her mother stood by the stove. She embraced her fondly then went back to her seat. "Thank you."

"For?"

"For all you do for us. You have been the heart of this family."

"God's been the heart of this family. If we put Him first in our lives...in each day, then things work out...through good or bad, things work out."

* * *

Dash was stuffed. Thanksgiving hadn't held so much promise to him since before his parents had passed away. It usually was just he and Aunt Katie. And while that had been nice and he was so thankful for her in his life, it was not the same as being in love and spending that special day with his aunt *and* Jaycee. The family had joined hands before dinner and each shared what they were thankful for. By the time it was his turn, he was speaking over a lump in his throat. *Thank you, God, for the kindness of friends and for Aunt Katie. Thank you for your son, Jesus, for His greatest sacrifice.*

Her family had been so inviting. He knew that his aunt and Jaycee's momma were close, he just had had no idea how much. It was like two ears of corn on the same stalk. Laughter filled the home as the family spied Dash's look at the Hamilton's traditional cranberry relish. He wasn't quite sure of what to think of the pink jellied mixture, only to find out it was cranberries and oranges mixed into raspberry Jell-O. Delicious! He had near enough finished the whole bowl himself and then they had produced another. A miracle.

He could feel the love in how the family treated each other, jokingly recalling Thanksgiving's past and teasing Jaycee on her black Friday sale obsession. She had been strangely quiet on that account...not having brought it up since the weekend fishing trip. But she laughed along at her family's ribbing.

He eyed her now, sitting next to him at the table with another helping of butternut squash on her plate; come to find out, her favorite vegetable. She saw his glance and reached a hand over to take his under the table. This Thanksgiving was special, beyond what he could have imagined....and he was grateful beyond any words could express, for what he *did* have this year...today. Especially for the love of one particular woman who he would swear he had loved since he was 8-year's old.

***

Jaycee had been in a deep sleep. Something was pulling her back though, away from the soft dreams and up into the world of tangled sheets and warm pillows. *Ting – Ting*. She squinted her eyes open, looking first at the glow of her alarm clock. *3:30*

She looked toward the sound coming from her window then struggled out from the covers, tripping as she went. Falling against the window with her outstretched hands, she pressed her nose to the glass. She could swear the grin started in her toes and worked its way up and throughout her whole body, where it landed on her lips.

Dash was there, a glowing flashlight at his feet and two mugs in one hand...waving at her with the other. She moved to her nightstand, flicked on her bedroom light and going back to the window, held up one finger.

Tossing clothes from her closet and drawers, she found her soft pink cashmere sweater and tan corduroys. Rushing into the bathroom, she flipped on the shower and while it was warming, brushed her hair and teeth. She washed up quickly and met Dash outside in the chilly morning air less than ten minutes later.

He was leaning against his Aunt Katie's car, grinning from ear to ear. "You needed a wingman?" He held his arms out to her. She stepped into them and he embraced her tightly, the smell of aftershave and cologne warming her senses.

She didn't speak for a moment, but closed her eyes, thanking God for the gift of this man. She stilled in his arms, and if truth be told, could've stayed there contentedly. *Black Friday.* Always one of her favorite adventures, it had loomed over her since quitting her job. She had been searching for whether to appease the shopping maven inside of her or listen to the reasoning voice. *No job. No job, Jaycee!*

Dash released her and opened the car door for Jaycee. She slid into the seat and he shut the door. The car had been running and was toasty warm. He got into the driver's side and lifted one of the mugs in the cup holder, passing it to her. He made no move to leave, but gathered his own coffee and sipped quietly, turning to face her.

"So. Am I or aren't I your old lady distractor for the day?"

She couldn't suppress a giggle. He could just about distract any female from an 80% off clearance sale. "Dash Matheson, what am I goin' to do with you?"

From where she sat, she was ready to tell him to drive them both to his apartment so she could near on spend the day in his arms. *But you're a good girl, Jaycee.* And sure enough, she was, but she had never found him more attractive than she did in this moment. *How did this love just keep building and building?*

She replaced her cup and put her hand out towards his in the space between them. He clasped it and slowly laced his fingers through hers. "I've got no job. Seems foolish."

She shook her head. She didn't know why it meant so much to her, this ritual. Sure it was a momentary thrill, but it was something more. Christmas. Giving and showing love as God showed His when He sent Jesus into the world.

"S'not foolish, Jaycee. Today is the only day we're guaranteed. God's been pressin' on me to live in it despite fires, death, sickness, a job or no job."

Jaycee nodded, sliding closer to him on the bench seat.

He put his hand to the side of her face, looking deeply into her eyes. "We may only be shoppin' with our pocket change and our heart's full of good intentions, but herein lies the treasure. We're together. It's life. Your life and mine. I want to share these moments with you; make enough memories to live a lifetime on."

Jaycee's heart flipped as his head inclined to kiss her. She whispered softly, "When life hands you lemons, you make.....fried chicken."

She could feel his smile on her mouth as his warm lips touched hers. Her lips parted slightly and she sighed into him, feeling him sober as their kiss became more intense. He pulled away briefly, "God, I love you, Jaycee."

"And I love you."

They joined lips again. The stars clung to the night and daylight was held at bay. The world suspended in the now and the motion of time paused. Then she pulled away, breathless, remaining in Dash's arms. Her eyes cleared as she opened them. A giggle burst forth and bubbled over. "The glass, Dash. Look at the windows."

She heard a chuckle rumble from his chest. "Steamed windows, steamed heart. I guess my charms are still workin'."

"Yes," Jaycee said, sliding a bit further away on the seat, "Let's go put those to good use, shall we?"

162

Winter

CHAPTER ONE

Jaycee stuck her right leg out, working the red tights into position on her torso. She smoothed the short green velvet skirt and fluffed the white puffy trim with her fingers. The man had said if the costume fit then she'd get the job. It was almost Christmas and she'd applied everywhere. This job had popped up in the classifieds just this morning.

With some trepidation, she turned toward the mirror in the makeshift dressing room. She focused on her head, tucking a length of bangs behind her ear and peering closer to studiously check her makeup. Her eyes wandered lower and she backed up. Might as well face the spectacle. She blinked. The yellow lacing across the front of the green shirt screamed up at her. Tiny red holly berries were stitched across the front. Jaycee

163

pulled up the sleeves slightly, the white edging tickling the backs of her hands.

She turned and reached for the accessories, fitting the curved shoe covers onto her feet, the bells tinkling lightly.

"Does it fit?" The man's voice sounded gruff through the curtain.

She bit her lip, hurriedly placing the pliable plastic ears at the sides of her head. She smashed the hat to her hair and yanked back the thin fabric, wanting to avoid her reflection.

The man looked up from where he sat putting on his tall black boots. His eyes crinkled as he looked at her and if Jaycee was 15 years younger, she'd think he was the real deal. Santa Claus.

"It fits!" he exclaimed. "You've got the job. Let's get you familiar with the camera next. Your first shift will be noon tomorrow. A schedule will be posted there." He pointed with a white gloved hand to a piece of paper taped to the makeshift wall.

Jaycee followed him over to a camera set up on a tripod. He explained which buttons to push and how to focus then had her stand in front of the camera. The blood rushed to Jaycee's head as he showed her the image on a small monitor set up on a nearby table.

"The parents can approve the picture or you can clear it and start again. See?" A different image of a blonde elf appeared. She nodded, her eyes traveling from the pointed ears to the curled-toe shoes on the screen.

He droned on about saving, printing, and filling out paper order forms. When he had finished, she thanked him politely and dashed back into the tiny dressing room. She wanted to laugh…maybe cry, but instead she got redressed, folded the outfit into her oversized bag, and fled to blend into the crowds at the mall.

***

"Don't laugh," Jaycee called out from the hallway.

"I won't," Dash promised. She had been quite mysterious about the job she had interviewed for earlier in the day.

"Can't say the same," Marcus yelled out, grinning at Dash from his spot on the carpet before the TV.

Dash threw a couch pillow at him, which Marcus caught one-handed and jammed beneath his elbows.

"Thanks!"

The lights from the tree twinkled onto the television screen as Jaycee's father hit the power button. He lifted his eyebrows at the two of them then yelled out, "We're waitin' on ya'."

"Is Momma in there?" Jaycee's voice carried.

Mrs. Hamilton rushed in from the kitchen and sat next to Dash. "Here," she called out.

A green foot appeared from around the doorframe followed by bright red stockings. Jaycee shook her foot dramatically, tinkling the tiny bell dangling from the top of the slipper. She appeared a moment later, half-grinning, but pink-faced before them.

Marcus let out a guffaw, which threatened to overflow in hilarity until Dash saw Mr. Hamilton give him a look. Marcus clamped a hand over his mouth then rolled his body across the rug as he tried to contain himself.

"Well," Jaycee's momma began, "You are just precious as can...be."

"I'm workin' at the mall, part-time." She cast her gaze down at her feet. Her bottom lip trembled, her small white teeth appearing then to bite down on it.

Dash moved from the couch and walked toward Jaycee, who still stood in the doorway.

Leaning forward, he cupped her elbow in his hand, his thumb caressing her through the fabric.

"Velvet?"

She nodded, her eyes now glued to his. A smile crept up and onto his lips; she was irresistible.

"Most beautiful Christmas elf I've ever seen."

He felt her breath release more than heard it. This must've been hard for her to do, this big reveal and the bigger picture, dress up in a mall full of people, many of whom she knew.

Her fingers curved over one of the elf ears and she pulled it off. With one ear on, she grinned. Marcus stilled from his merriment and in fascination, sat up, "Can I try 'em?"

"Don't break them, okay?" He nodded as she tossed the plastic ears to him. He fit them to his own, running from the room to look in the hall mirror.

"So, workin' for Saint Nick, are ya?" Jaycee's Dad asked. "What's your schedule?"

Jaycee padded across the carpet to stand near the tree, taking the hat from her head and nodding. "Tomorrow at noon. Not sure of my regular days yet. Expect I'll find out then."

Dash took in the picture of her with the decorated tree behind her and the brilliant white star high above her head.

Even to him, her skirt seemed tiny on her petite frame and when he thought of her going out in public in it, he wanted to yank it down by the puffy trim. If he hadn't had a girl elf infatuation before, he expected he had one now.

***

Back in her comfy black sweatshirt and yoga pants, Jaycee walked back into the living room. Dash had gotten a movie for the night. Having anticipated her family watching with them, she was surprised when it was just Dash on the couch waiting for her with a big bowl of popcorn before him and the remote in his hand.

"Your folks went to bed."

"Was Daddy okay?" She settled herself beside him and into the crook of his arm.

"Seemed so."

"He's still unsteady. He's better, just not...not the same."

"It might take more time or different meds. You just don't know. We can just hope and pray."

"You're right. You're always right," she grinned and pinched his gut playfully. "It gets annoying."

He went on the offensive and grabbed her hand, holding it firmly and pulling her closer to tickle her under her arm.

She laughed and whispered loudly, "Okay, okay—truce!"

He released her and Jaycee sat back, breathless. She hated to be tickled and he knew it.

She wanted to be mad at him, but she couldn't. Truth was, she was glad to see him so relaxed. Work had picked up for him and he had decided to hire another mechanic. She knew it wasn't an easy decision for him; almost admitting he wouldn't be back under a car anytime soon.

She slid the remote from between his fingers as she leaned in and planted a kiss on his cheek. She placed the popcorn bowl into his hands. "Fair trade?"

"Is this how you get yer way with me, woman? Plyin' me with kisses and food?"

"My elfen charms," she said offhandedly, clicking through the menu screen to find the play button.

"So….," Dash began.

She waited. She knew she looked foolish. An elf. She shouldn't have reminded him. She held her breath and waited for his words. She looked from the TV into his face. He wiggled his eyebrows at her, a gleam coming into his eyes. "You get to keep the outfit?"

Jaycee knew that look. Things were getting serious in that department. They had both agreed to wait, to stop and forgo the hormones. For the time being, they'd spend more time at her house than at his apartment alone.

His eyes were on her lips and she felt drawn to him like red and white on a candy cane. Her finger hit the play button, but she slid the bowl from his hands and back onto the table then sat herself gently across his lap. Dash took her face in his hands and kissed her deeply.

"Oh, Jaycee," he whispered.

She kissed him back and moved reluctantly from his lap. "I love you."

"I love you too." He breathed out.

They remained apart for almost half the movie...until reason returned and the fire had banked between them.

CHAPTER TWO

It was all fun and games until the reality of putting herself out there for public humiliation came home to roost. It being mid-day Thursday, the mall wasn't overflowing with people yet. Jaycee walked through the brightly lit corridors, eyeing the bows and sparkles in one of her favorite store's window. She checked her watch and walked more quickly through the food court to duck behind the canvas walls of the tent. She waved a greeting to an already dressed Santa.

"Right on time. We open in ten minutes. All dressed?"

"Yes...Santa," she answered, allowing herself a small smile while she removed and hung up her black trench coat. She sat on a nearby stool and worked at the zipper on her boots. Pulling an extra pair of shoes from her purse once her feet were free, she put those on and the green elf coverings over them.

"Names Jack, but stick with Santa. That way we won't make any mistakes in front of the kiddos," he said, winking.

She nodded then looked around for a spot to place her purse.

"There's a locker under the table there. Here, put it in mine. Tomorrow, might want to bring your own lock." He indicated the two other doors without locks while he twirled his combination. She tucked her purse in with what looked like a few watches and Jack's street clothes. *Reality. Santa was just a man.* Let's hope this boss didn't turn out like the last one.

"Grab your hours for the week then meet me out front."

He grabbed the camera and tripod and disappeared through a flap in the fabric.

Jaycee stuck the plastic elf ears to her head by feel then went to the mirror to adjust the hat.

She tugged at her sleeves and wiggled her shoes, bells tinkling quietly. She studied herself carefully. *A circle of red at each cheek would really make this outfit.* Nodding to herself with a sheepish grin. Go all in or go home. And the second wasn't an appealing option. She was so bored of being around the house for days on end. This was just what the doctor, or God, or some strange force of nature had ordered.

She snatched a piece of paper off the table and wrote her hours down for the next several days. Prime shopping time. She inwardly started to cringe. So much attention.

Straightening, she gave herself a pep talk. She would further mask the real Jaycee. This was an adventure. Fun, even. *Yeah, that's what it was going to be. Julia Cozetta Hamilton, you quit two jobs in the span of a few short months. Time to suck it up and pay the fiddler.* Maybe God could even use this itty bitty job for good and His glory and will.

175

Stoic and with a prayer on her lips, she carried a stack of order forms along with several pens to the front of the makeshift room and out onto the stage of the cordoned off area of Santa's workshop. A red throne for Santa sat center with a tree to the right lit with colored lights and big silver and gold bulbs. Surrounding the tree and on both sides of the chair were brightly wrapped packages with enormous bows.

Jaycee descended the stage, bending down as she went to adjust the red carpet that led up the stairs and down the aisle. Jack had set the camera up and was fooling with the wires to the tiny TV-like screen. She plopped the forms on the table beside it.

"We're almost set. Remember how to run this?"

She nodded mutely, though watched as he went through the steps again.

"We take cash and credit cards. This machine here, you swipe the cards and they can enter their pin. Got it?"

And so the day began. Her first soiree into retail.

***

Dash knew it was Jaycee's first day on the job. He imagined she'd be flustered enough without getting a visit from him, so he circumspectly avoided the food court until last. He tucked the tiny box securely in his pocket then made a detour, peering out from a nearby clothing boutique to check on her.

He had wanted to hold it in his hands and know it was real. Looking online was one thing, but was so removed from the reality of how he felt. He had found the perfect cut, just for her, at the mall jewelry store.

"May I help you find something?" A saleswoman came up behind him and asked.

He had a girl's sweater in his hand. He looked down at it, his face flooding with heat. Fuzzy white and black fabric with rhinestones shined up at him.

"Uh-no." He placed it back on the rack by the store window, his attention on the woman. "Not for me…just, well. My girlfriend works over there. Her first day."

The saleswoman peered over his shoulder, her eyes widening. "With Santa?"

"Yes, she's the elf."

"Checking in on her, are you?"

"I was shoppin' and…"

The woman glanced at his empty hands. "No success? Perhaps I can show you something." Her voice trailed away.

He consciously patted the breast pocket of his coat and smiled, turning to glance back towards Santa's workshop, his eyes searching for Jaycee.

"Ohhhh...I see," the woman's slight smile widened. "What's her name? Your special elf."

"Jaycee."

"Well, I won't tell a soul and I wish you the best with your Christmas surprise."

"Th-thank you..."

"Nancy...Nancy Owens. I own this shop. Just opened a few months ago."

"Thanks, Nancy. I'm Dash Mattheson." He made to leave the store then added, "If you're a prayin' woman, mind throwin' me a few prayers for the big moment?"

"I am and I will. You follow the Lord's leading, you'll do fine."

***

Jaycee dug her fingers into her hair, forcing the strands apart one by one. Her replacement, Lisa, had shown up a few minutes before the end

179

of her shift and had gotten Jaycee some ice from one of the food vendors.

She slid the frozen cube over the wad of gum at the side of her head, working it back and forth then picked at the sticky mound. Try as she might, she couldn't rightly remember which sandy-haired, brunette, chubby-faced, bright-eyed child it had come from. Was it thrown, landing on her arm and working its way up? Maybe from bending over and lifting up one of the wiggly bodies into Santa's lap?

She shivered and dropped the melting sliver into the trash.

Turning towards the coat tree, she glanced beside and behind it for her coat. It was gone!

She stuck her head back out through the curtain, catching Lisa's attention who came onto the platform.

"My coat's gone. Did you see it? Long black wool."

Lisa shook her head. "Can't say as I have. Been some thefts in the mall though. That's why we got the lockers."

Jaycee nodded her thanks and ducked back into the makeshift room. Looking down at her elf costume, she cringed thinking about the walk to the car. Not to mention getting something to eat. Her stomach responded with a low growl. Keeping her flats on, she tucked the shoe covers in her purse and carried her boots under her arm. She took a deep breath and exited into the busy foot traffic of the mall.

The food court was packed. Jaycee made her way to stand in line at Hunan Fortune, stoically focusing her attention on the menu before her. Soon enough it was her turn. She took her food and drink atop a brown tray and slid into a nearby table. A little girl danced to the right of her as she opened her plastic-encased fork and knife.

Sniffing the Chinese food appreciatively and with eyes open to the food and crowds, and the little girl dancing closer and closer to where she sat, Jaycee said a silent prayer of thanks. A lady who Jaycee assumed to be the little girl's mother sat at a table in deep conversation with an older man with a long gray beard.

Was he accosting her? He certainly looked homeless. Jaycee focused on the little girl with her long black hair in tight pigtails. Straight bangs hung low across her eyebrows. Brown eyes lit up and her cheeks flushed as she eyed Jaycee up and down.

Glancing back at her mother, the little girl twirled closer and leaned in. "Are you an elf?"

Jaycee leaned in just as conspiratorially, "I am, but just at Christmas time. Otherwise, I'm an ordinary woman."

The girl seemed to accept this information straightaway, grinning widely and hopping on one foot then the other.

"And elves like Chinese food?" she asked loudly.

Jaycee saw the little girl's mother glance at her and then at Jaycee.

"We do. You can't get it up at the North Pole."

"You live in the North Pole?" Her eyes became round saucers.

"Only this time of year. Otherwise, I live not too far from here."

Jaycee saw the old man get up and shuffle away. The little girl's mother came to stand near her daughter.

"We're sorry to bother you." Her arm drawing the girl close, who wiggled free and bounded off again, dancing on her tiptoes.

"It's fine. No bother. The outfit, I'm findin', tends to fascinate the little ones."

"Yes, I can see that it would. You work with Santa?" The woman nodded her head towards Santa's photo area.

"Yes. Today was my first day."

The woman's eyes seemed to light up and her mouth formed an "O". Extending her hand, she introduced herself, "I'm Nancy Owens. I own Heaven Sent, the boutique at the corner. If you need anything while you're here, let me know."

"I just love your store!"

"Thank you so much. I'm not there as often as I'd like but it's been doing well the short time it's been open."

"Can I ask you a question, working here longer than I, you may know."

The woman nodded.

"Heard tell of any thefts lately? My coat was stolen."

The woman nodded. "Mall security's been working on it. Want to blame the homeless, but those poor souls aren't the ones stealing from what I've gathered." Her eyes slid towards the man she had been speaking to. She raised her hand to him as their eyes met. He was by the trash receptacle, buttoning his threadbare coat against the burgeoning cold that had descended on the area. "They roust them daily from the mall for loitering. For some, a quick jaunt through the mall, even if it's from being run out by security, is all the warmth they feel most days."

Jaycee's eyes followed the old man as he made his way to the quad doors of the mall entrance. She cast a glance at her overly full plate of food. The woman's hand came to rest on Jaycee's shoulder momentarily. "Never you mind. I've come up with a little plan to give them some comfort this Christmas. Maybe you'd want to help?"

"I'd be happy to," she replied, meeting the woman's eyes, a warm feeling spreading into the pit of her stomach.

"This is Rebecca, by the way. Tell her how old you are, Rebecca." She said, addressing the little girl.

Rebecca held up her hand, concentrating on the pudgy fingers displayed then counted them slowly, 1-2-3.

CHAPTER THREE

Dash gathered his wits about him as he drove to Jaycee's parent's home. It was 40 degrees and colder than usual for December. He flipped the truck's ancient heater on, the whirring and instant heat causing his nerves to ease. He concentrated on the tiny winding road, flanked on both sides with dense trees which lead to the Hamilton's small farm.

Arriving, he parked in the driveway beside both of her parent's vehicles. Marcus would still be in school this time of day. He exhaled and knocked at the front door. Mrs. Hamilton answered with a dishtowel in hand. "Well, hi there, Dash. Jaycee's at work."

His mouth went dry as he willed it to open.

She smiled at him and clasped his arm to draw him into the house. "I expect you know that though. Is there something we can help you with?"

"I-I'm in the mind to have a talk with Mr. Hamilton." He met her eyes with his own, the crinkles deepening as her smile widened.

"With the way the cold's pressin' in, he should be in from the fields soon for coffee." She led the way to the kitchen, glancing back to be sure he followed. "Would you like to take the thermos and mugs out there?"

Dash nodded, steadying the swinging door with his hand and coming to stand near the kitchen table. Jaycee's momma worked quickly with the already steaming coffee. She tightened the lid firmly then handed a thermos and two mugs to Dash.

"You're all set. I'll have some hot blueberry muffins comin' from the oven shortly. Ya'll come on back for some when you're through."

"Thank you, ma'am."

Dash nearly tripped over his feet as he went out the back and through the screened in porch. The thermos reassured him. The heat sank against his hand. He tried to still the clanging of the ceramic mugs, but the sound seemed to play in tune as the wind picked up and blew, entangling the branches of the nearby trees. He rounded their barn and headed for the fenced in corral. Two horses flicked their tails and neighed quietly as he passed.

He followed the fence line to the end and kept moving forward. It was here the wire fencing started, where the Hamilton's kept their cattle. Mr. Hamilton appeared from over a slope in the pasture, heading his way. Dash held up a hand in greeting and halted.

"Dash. How are you son?" Mr. Hamilton called.

"Fine, Sir. Came to have a talk."

Jaycee's father nodded to the coffee as they both rounded and walked back towards the house. "And I expect the Mrs. sent us fortification."

"Yes, sir."

Once on the porch, Dash set the cups down on a small table then poured the coffee and handed a steaming mug to Mr. Hamilton who had settled himself in a chair, surveying the pasture and mares.

"Don't know what will become of it."

"Sir?"

"The farm. Jaycee's never been overly fond of the dirt. You know that. And Marcus, darned if I know if he'll want to spend his life toilin' the land and raisin' cattle for profit."

"I imagine he'll be keen on the idea as he grows," Dash commented, looking out at the patches of brown grass in the field and the troughs of hay and water. A pitchfork and shovel lay against the chipping red paint of the barn. A peace pressed on him. Living off the land, now that was a feat. He looked sideways, to the east of the house. Mrs. Hamilton's gardens stretched out over several hundred feet and beyond that, dormant skeletons of fruit and nut trees.

He dragged his gaze back to Jaycee's father, feeling his quiet expectation as he sipped his coffee.

"I'm sure you're wonderin' what I needed to talk to you about."

"A mite."

"Jaycee and I've been around each other since we were kids." He gripped the mug tighter, forming the words slowly. "It's been a short time, us dating, but...I'm in love with her. I want to ask her to be my wife." He had been sitting rigid and with the last sentence, he eased back on the cushioned wicker chair, relief flooding his body now that the declaration had been made.

Mr. Hamilton remained silent, his eyes moving across Dash's face.

He continued. "And a man knows. She's the one. I want to ask her at Christmas."

"And if I object or say no."

"Then I'll respect your decision...and wait."
Dash wanted to stand and pace, but he willed
himself to meet Mr. Hamilton's keen stare.

"She's so far away from where she needs to
be, in life, I mean. And knowin' what she wants to
do. She's an elf at the mall, for goodness sake."

"She is. And she's taken the job despite
what must be an embarrassment to herself and her
pride. Jaycee can do anything she sets her mind to.
When she decides what it is she wants to do for the
next 5, 20, 30 years, I'll be right there with her
supporting her decisions."

"And if it's college?"

"Then we'll get her there."

"What if she wants to leave again? Move
from Twain?"

"I expect we'll have those conversations,
Mr. Hamilton, Sir."

Silence descended over the porch. Had he
blown it? Maybe it was too soon, yet his gut and
his heart knew it to be right.

"It's Jeb."

"What?"

"Call me Jeb. I'm not ready for "Dad" yet."

***

"What time is the movie?" Jaycee asked, arranging the chicken on the platter and scooping up the rolls with her other hand. With a flourish she exited the kitchen and deposited the meal on Dash's small dining table.

"9 o'clock."

Jaycee lit the bright red tapers. "Perfect. We can take hot chocolate and drive through town to look at the lights before it starts. Come eat."

Dash rubbed his belly hungrily, limping slightly as he crossed the room and sat at her bidding. "You spoil me, woman."

"Just so," she grinned back at him, piling the barbeque chicken high on a fluffy bun and handing him his plate. "Don't forget some salad."

"Rabbit food!"

"It's good for you. Made the ranch homemade too."

He reached over, pulling the dressing closer and poured a hefty spoonful on top of his chicken sandwich.

"That's – not what I meant."

Dash grabbed her hand loosely then and bowed his head. She sighed happily, following his lead and closed her eyes.

"Dear God, we are thankful for this food and each other. Direct our steps. Help us show the world Your love. In Jesus' name we pray, Amen."

Her hand grew warm as the room stilled and he held her within his gentle grip. Jaycee squinted an eye open. He was silently praying. The food forgotten, Jaycee's mind quieted on thoughts of Dash. *What a blessing this man is to my life.* A man after God's own heart and what more could she want? Did she still yearn for more?

No. She didn't know where God wanted her work-wise, but there was a contentment now. Whether in a career or just a job, God had a plan. Nancy's mention of helping with a dinner for the homeless interested Jaycee. Fear plagued her in some respects, yet she knew, as she had learned from exploring the Bible each morning before her feet touched the floor, that God would go before and behind her, a constant shadow of protection.

Dash opened his eyes and turned her hand over in his. He pulled it to his lips, kissing her gently. "Thanks for dinner, love."

"You're welcome," she said, blinking back faint tears. *A precious man.*

He released her hand and attacked his sandwich. In between bites, he complimented her cooking. "Best sandwich ever." He cocked his head to one side. "Hey, how about bein' a chef?"

She loved cooking for him and more recently for the family, but full-time? It was something she needed to pray over. "I'll be helpin' cook at a homeless dinner Christmas eve."

"Where's this?"

"I met a woman today, owns a store in the mall. She's organizing it."

"Sounds like a worthy cause. You know I'll help too, if you all can use me."

She nodded.

"How was your day? I didn't want to bring it up until you had a chance to relax."

"Dramatic...but good."

"Dramatic?"

"Kids squealing, crying, crawling, running, jumping. Wow, I'm pure wore out." She sighed dramatically and rolled her eyes.

"Good practice," he said, grinning.

Jaycee about dropped her salad fork. "Excuse me?"

"You know, for someday. Kids."

"Maybe we should talk about that after this 'North Pole season' of my life."

196

"Ya' want them, right?"

Jaycee looked at him, contemplating. "Sure. You?"

"In time, yes." Dash grinned then, taking another helping of chicken and added, "As long as their momma can cook."

CHAPTER FOUR

Jaycee was starting to get the flow of the job. Chat with parents, put the children at ease, lead the way to Santa, help them sit on his lap, picture taking, order form.

Try as she might, it was hard to separate the little ones from the conversation she had with Dash the night before. The children's hopes shone bright this Christmas with visions of toys from the big man himself and inevitably from their adoring parents. Good gifts, like God longed to give to each one of His children. And ultimately had with the gift of His own son. A true miracle to be celebrated.

Each child's face held a sparkle from Dash's eyes, the tilt of his head, or a dimple so like his in the curve of a chubby cheek. Their long lashes beckoned Jaycee and she found herself holding little hands a moment longer and her heart being tugged from its place by their tears or laughter.

Break time came quickly at midday. Jaycee hooked the velvet rope across the entrance and removed the camera from the tripod. She and Santa had 35 minutes for lunch. He had left already. She noted his jacket still on the coat tree, realizing he was probably at the food court where she was headed. She sidled closer to make sure her old down coat was still there, shifting his in the process. It swiftly fell to the floor and in relief, she saw hers had been beneath it.

She reached to pick up his jacket when something shiny slid from the pocket. It looked like a diamond and aquamarine bracelet. The tags were still attached from Battersby Jewelers. *Wow, somebody was going to have a good Christmas.* She tucked the jewelry back into the pocket and rehung the jacket.

Twirling the combination lock, Jaycee grabbed her wallet from her purse. Like it or not, she was not changing just to get lunch. She momentarily thought on the bracelet, wondering if

Jack knew about the thefts at the mall. Maybe he'd be more apt to tuck it away in his locker if he did, like the watches she'd seen. An uneasy feeling crept over her as she left the enclosure and headed for the food court.

Deep in thought as she walked, her wallet slipped from her hand, falling open and scattering change across the wide expanse before the first fast food counter. She bent down, twisting demurely so the small skirt wouldn't hike up. Leaning forward, she reached for the last two quarters and overheard a couple talking with a security guard.

"Pandering. He had a scruffy beard, dirty as can be."

"We'll take care of it, ma'am." The security guard said, grabbing his walkie-talkie from his belt.

"You can't even come into the mall without one of them with a hand out." The woman's companion said gruffly, sniffing his nose in distaste.

"Which entrance was it?"

"Near Kid's Corner."

The officer continued to assure them they would take care of it. Jaycee sidled off the floor and walked quickly to the Kid's Corner mall entrance. She whipped open one of the double doors then threaded through the next set in between a woman and her son. The child yanked on his mother's hand and pointed to her. She briefly smiled at the boy as she passed them.

The cold wind knocked her back a moment and she clutched at the thin velvet fabric at her arms. Her eyes searched for the man the couple had described. It was the same elderly man who had been talking with Nancy Owens yesterday in the food court. His hands were stuffed in his pockets and he leaned against the side of the brick wall, as if trying to avoid the wind. Jaycee said a prayer and hesitantly approached him.

Contemplating the cash in her wallet, she spoke. "I—I overheard a couple complaining to a security guard. Thought I should warn you."

He had a woolen hat pulled low over his ears and looked at her through his weathered wrinkled face, his piercing, surprisingly alert eyes little slits. Shuffling from his position, he started off towards the parking lot. She followed after him as her shivering hands worked at the clasp on her wallet, pulling five dollars from between its depths.

"Sir, Sir…" she called.

He stopped and faced her again. "I'm mighty obliged you told me. God bless you, girlie."

"Here. For you." Jaycee pushed the money towards him. "God bless you too. I—I'm sorry it's so dreadfully cold of late. Do you have somewhere to go?"

"There's a shelter. Most nights there's enough room. And by the tracks we build a fire." He dipped his head as he reached for the money. "Thanks for the warning and this."

She watched him go. He reached the edge of the parking lot and disappeared into the trees. A shadow fell across her as a man came to stand behind her, his voicing booming in her ears and causing her to jump. "What do you think you're doing?"

Jaycee turned, her temper flaring. The security guard from the mall, she should have guessed, and his partner was just exiting the building. "Me?"

"Did *you* warn him we were comin'?"

Jaycee jutted her chin forward and met the man's angry gaze with her own. "I did and I gave him some money for food to boot."

"Food!" The man snorted. "More'n likely he'll have drunk it by dinner."

"That's between him and God. You should be ashamed of yourself. That man has nowhere to go."

"His own fault. And I've got nothin' to be ashamed of."

"Maybe you should worry more about the thefts in the mall. My coat was taken the other day!" Jaycee declared, stomping her feet as she bounded back towards the mall.

"Another reason to clear the riff raff. That's *my job*. I suggest you get back to yours." He yelled at her back.

***

Four more days until Christmas Eve. Not much time to plan. While Jaycee was adjusting to her new job, Dash'd been trying to think of the perfect way to ask her to be his wife. Didn't it have to be magical, like time standing still? He'd heard tell enough of women needing to look back on the memory when things were overwhelming as children entered the picture with laundry, house cleaning, cooking, and even working full time. One thing was for sure, he was going to help shoulder the load. That is, if she accepted.

He pushed his shoulders back, standing up from behind his desk. The parts order had been called in and the next few days were full up of appointments. Having hired a new mechanic had helped with the workload and Dash was concentrating on the marketing end. He enjoyed his time coming up with new ad ideas to get the word out about the place. It helped that his aunt Katie was helping at the front desk. It gave her a purpose, she said.

He walked out into the small waiting area where she was tapping away on the computer keyboard. She looked up and waved to him. "Want some coffee, I just made it fresh."

"No, but thanks. Thought I'd run over to Carlson's. Last minute shopping." He shuffled his feet, contemplating asking her for ideas. By some miracle, something had to come to him and soon.

She didn't seem to notice his delay, concentrating on the screen. He shook his head and left. *Dear Lord in heaven, give me some inspiration to make this moment special for Jaycee.*

Carlson's, the local five and dime, was crowded. Dash stood amidst the bustle of people in the small space, looking over heads towards the shelves and counters stuffed with bright holiday ornaments, snow globes, framed pictures of snowy landscapes, and trinkets. Nothing struck Dash with an ah-ha idea so he spent a few minutes browsing the other side of the store.

About giving up, he moved to leave when something caught his eyes. It was a tiny stuffed bear thrown into a bin of little girl's hair ribbons. He lifted it and placed it in his hand where it fit top to bottom from the tips of Dash's fingers to the end of his palm. The gentleman bear was covered in soft cream fur and dressed in red trousers with a tiny shirt with a drumstick stitched on the front. Dash grinned.

* * *

It was the third meeting that Nancy and Jaycee had had about the dinner on Christmas Eve. They met in the food court. Nancy'd asked her church to help with the evening and the cooking would be done by a church member who was a chef. A menu had been roughed out with traditional ham, turkeys, stuffing, mashed potatoes, sweet potato casserole, green beans cooked in bacon grease, and plenty of cookies and pies for the celebration.

Dinner would be served to the homeless and less fortunate families in the area at a local VFW who had donated the space. Jaycee had enlisted Dash's help along with her mother and brother to help set up and serve.

"Do you know anyone who plays the piano?" Nancy asked, jotting something down in her notebook and looking across at her.

"My momma used to. What do you have in mind?" She took a last bite quickly, her break almost over. She'd brought the salad from home.

The food court prices were really eating into her upcoming paycheck.

"Thought we'd have some lyrics printed, sing a few carols."

"I'll ask Momma which Christmas songs she knows, then we can print them. How many songs?"

"Three I think would be perfect."

Jaycee nodded, packing up the plastic Tupperware bowl into her lunch sack. "How's Rebecca feeling?" Nancy's energetically bright daughter had been sick with the stomach flu the day before.

"Keeping things down. Tom's home with her for a few hours while I tie up last minute plans and check on the store."

"So glad she's better." Jaycee found herself looking forward to seeing the little girl. Her joy for life was infectious. She also was a good distraction. Things had turned strange working with Jack. Maybe it was her overactive imagination, but he'd been silent and brooding ever since Jaycee had mentioned the thefts and the bracelet having fallen from his coat pocket. It's not like she could alert the security guards; she was persona non grata where they were concerned.

Maybe Nancy could help her. "Hear anything else about the thefts in the mall?"

Nancy stood, jamming the paper and pen into her overstuffed purse. They walked towards Heaven Sent and Jaycee's work. "Jewelry's been the main thing stolen. Though I heard tell of some high end clothing items disappearing and personnel's belongings from out of the stores."

"What kind of jewelry?" Jaycee asked, digging for answers.

"Watches, rings, bracelets, necklaces." Nancy made to part ways.

Jaycee was unsure and hovered, mid-step towards the tent enclosure. She still had questions and wanted to confide in Nancy over her fears about Jack. She'd become even more suspicious when she'd seen him standing by the velvet ropes earlier in the day accepting something from a man dressed in black.

"I have my suspicions." Jaycee blurted out, almost to Nancy's back. Nancy backpedaled and returned to where Jaycee stood.

"What do you mean?" Looking her full in the face and grabbing her arm.

Jaycee felt ridiculous. She really had no proof. No cause to talk. "Just with Santa…he acts off. Slippery is the word that comes to mind. Also saw some things in his locker."

"Did you tell security?"

"I will if I see anything else. I expect the items are gone by now. Probably just Christmas presents and my crazy sixth sense is off kilter."

"Jaycee, don't go playing hero. If you think he's a thief, you never know, he could be worse. And around children to boot."

She nodded and squeezed Nancy's hand. "I'll be sure and report anything from here on out." Jaycee hadn't thought about him with the kids.

CHAPTER FIVE

Dash entered the Hamilton's kitchen and into a whirling storm of baking. Jaycee sat on a high stool next to the middle island with flour on her cheeks and red jam heaping from the spoon in her hand. He moved closer. She smelled of vanilla and berries. He leaned in to give her a kiss on her nose and she smiled up at him, clearly in her element. Any tension she had shown the past few nights after work seemed to have eased from her shoulders and face as she concentrated on pushing a finger into the top of a cookie and pushing jelly into the hole.

He went to the sink and washed his hands, then pulled a stool up to the other side of the island. "I'm all yours. Where can I help?"

"We're splitting the thumb print cookies and shortbreads up between the dinner tomorrow night and gifts for neighbors. There's tons of dough." She made a kissy face at him, puckering her lips. "Do you think you can get one of the bowls out of the fridge and put confectioner's sugar on the counter surface?"

"I am at your beck and call."

"And I love you for it." She stood to slide the two finished sheet pans of jam-filled cookies into the oven. Leaning over into a cabinet, she pulled some cooling racks from beneath, setting them up on the counter by the stove.

"We all set then, for tomorrow night? I'll meet ya' at the VFW right after work, 4:00 okay?"

"Perfect. I'm supposed to get off by 3:00, so Nancy and I'll be there. Momma's comin' with Marcus 'round that time too."

"We servin'? Cookin'? Do you know?"

"There should be plenty of help with Nancy's church pitchin' in. The chef's makin' most things beforehand. I expect he's as busy as we are tonight." She cocked her head to the side, watching him as he worked the firm dough with the rolling pin. "We'll set up the chafing dishes, rewarm, serve, and keep the food stocked."

Dash heard music playing from somewhere in the house. She must've seen the question in his eyes. "Momma's gonna play a few Christmas carols. Can't wait. It's been a while since she's taken the time. It's a blessing."

The chords of Silent Night washed over them both. Jaycee drew closer to him, licking the jam from one of her fingers. Her eyes softened. He pushed the stool further from the counter and she sat on his lap, momentarily tucking her head beneath his chin. Her soft sigh twisted at his insides and his mind wandered to the little box tucked inside his jacket in the hallway closet.

***

Why'd life have to be so complicated? Truer words it was perfect most days, especially moments, hours with Dash. But being yanked back to reality on a daily basis by the worries of this world were pulling on Jaycee's last patient nerve and the good Lord knew she hadn't many of those.

Jaycee saw the man again talking with Jack. He slipped something into the white glove covered hands of Jack's Santa outfit, who pocketed whatever it was and headed back into the enclosure. Jaycee followed him a short time later, seeing him step away from the lockers. Well, enough was enough.

"What's goin' on?" She said, glaring at the man, her imagination and gander up.

"Excuse me?" He went to the mirror calmly, adjusting his red hat and the spectacles at his nose.

"I am well aware that man is passin' you stolen items from the stores 'round here. And I can sure enough prove it. Open your locker!"

Despite the whiskers plastered to Jack's face, she saw the man's face redden. He stepped towards her threateningly. A tingle of fear crawled up her spine and she faltered. Glancing back, she saw the gap in the tent was open wide enough to see the morning walker's club stroll past.

"My dear, I could silence you in the course of one second." He flexed his fingers before him, watching her through hooded eyes and glancing toward the opening.

Jaycee raised her voice, "You wouldn't dare!"

The man's bulk was almost obscene but with the swiftness of a cat, he came at her reaching toward her neck. Jaycee stumbled back and tripped over a spare wrapped present at her feet. She crawled quickly towards the tent door and stopped short at a pair of dirt encrusted boots at the opening.

Jaycee breathed out a warning to whoever was there, "Run! He's dangerous."

She saw the boots with their untied broken laces step over her. There was scuffling and grunting behind her as the two men fought. Jaycee ducked her head and prayed. A sharp yelp split the air and then a rush of air blew across her hair.

Unshed tears escaped Jaycee's eyes as she cautioned a glance behind her. The man with the ragged boots, it was the old man. He had come to her rescue! And now he was lying in a heap on the floor behind her. She crawled over to him on her knees.

A crowd had started to gather at the tent flap and a woman came in, putting a hand at Jaycee's back and going to kneel by the man's prostrate frame.

Jaycee looked around. Jack must've taken off out the opposite way. She heaved a sigh, letting the tears flow freely. A moment later security was there, and among them, the same guard who had given her such a hard time outside the mall.

She hiccupped, trying to control her crying. "Santa—Santa was the thief. He and another man. Check the locker, he stashed something there a while ago and I confronted him." She nodded towards the old man, lying still. Gritting her teeth, she fell at the old man's side. "Th—this man saved my life."

***

The VFW was off a side street near downtown. It was an old warehouse of a building with an ancient kitchen, but, Dash expected, big enough for their purposes. When he arrived, decorating was in high gear. There was an organ in the main room with long tables and chairs encompassing the entire floor space. Red and green paper draped each table, along with greenery and a battery-operated candle in the center of each. A large, round Christmas tree had been pushed into a corner where its lights flashed along to some imagined tune.

He glanced quickly around the room for Jaycee. She had called him earlier, on the tail end of tears, telling him what had happened at the mall. He'd wanted to drop everything and rush over, but her parents had been called and she was heading home in their car to take a hot shower and change. Dash had urged her to try to rest before the evening.

He knew she was safe, but he'd wanted to see her, hold her. Assure her it wouldn't happen again. He'd protect her. But how, in a world that was becoming increasingly more dangerous and unsound? His breathing sounded loud in his ears as headed for the swinging doors of the kitchen. She'd be back there. *God hadn't failed him. She was fine.* His heart squeezed at the thought of what could have happened. But she was okay. And that was all that mattered.

She was standing next to an oversized boiling pot. Her blonde hair was pulled away from her face. She met his gaze across the crowd of people, the noise dimming as he looked into her eyes. Tiny shadows smudged beneath them and weariness showed across her face. He crossed to her, one hand encircling her waist as he came to stand before her. He bent forward, nuzzling her cheek, oblivious to anyone around them. "I've missed you. Couldn't stop worryin'."

"I'm okay," she said quietly, cupping his chin in one of her hands to hold his face still next to hers. "Jobless again, but okay." Her grin twisted as tears appeared in her eyes.

"Can you take a break for a minute?"

She nodded, turning the heat beneath the pot lower and wiping her hands on the towel hanging on the stove front. She grabbed his hand and led him out the back door, which was propped open to allow cool air to circulate in the hot kitchen.

He was flushed already. He couldn't breathe. Couldn't think of anything but proposing. He had to do it. But was this it, the perfect moment? Maybe he should allow her to heal. To grow...without him. Dare he put the burden of becoming his wife on top of all her other cares now? What if she said no? Worse, what if their relationship ended completely if he asked?

***

The sky was darkening already. The back parking lot held few cars. Jaycee led the way over to the tree line, a picnic table tucked in beneath an ancient elm. She needed this time, away from the noise, the heat, and the chaos.

She was so grateful things had turned out the way they had. And even more so that Clem Turner, the old man, would be okay. He was admitted to Mercy Hospital for the night, tucked safely into a warm bed.

"The old man, Clem...can we go see him after. Maybe bring him a plate of food for Christmas Eve?"

"Nothin' more I want to do than thank that man for saving you." Dash sat on the top of the picnic table with Jaycee kneeling on the bench facing him.

"It's funny. Christmas used to be all about the presents. Now...now it's about the people I love and..." She nodded towards the VFW, "those who have so much less but still have joy in their hearts. That certainly is how to keep Christmas all year 'round."

He wrapped her in his arms and pulled her close. The wind caught and snagged at her loose sweater, pulling on the ends. His face was in her hair. She closed her eyes, willing him to move closer, closer ever still.

"God gave us the greatest gift. Jesus' life, which overcame the sting of death. We can have joy...no matter the circumstance." She felt him gulp. He moved to look into her face. "I wasn't quite truthful. There is *one other thing* I can think of that I'd like to do more."

She opened her eyes then and noticed from the shelter of the reaching branches of the old tree, the dancing flakes of snow beginning to fall around them.

"Snow! It's been years!" Dash's eyes lit up and she could swear he had tears in them. "Are you okay?"

"I can't imagine if somethin' happened to you today, Jaycee. You are the love of my life." He removed a hand from behind her back and put it inside his coat. "I got you...this." He pulled something small and furry out and handed it to her. She gasped. It was an exquisite bear with jointed arms and legs. She pulled it closer to her face, looking at the t-shirt and embroidered picture of a fried drumstick.

"It's adorable. Where did you ever find it?" She hugged it close, feeling it's soft warm fur.

"God led me to it...and to you. I love you more than anyone or anything on this earth. I'll be with you here in Twain, Georgia, New York City, or wherever you think we need to be. I'll support your dreams and help you reach new heights, but I want to do it as your husband. Jaycee will you marry me?"

The world was a snow globe and she was the princess inside. Yet it wasn't a fairy tale. Her one true love was real. God had seen fit to send Dash to her. And wherever He led, Dash would be there. For an eternity, for the now and the then, for the coming years, and the happy ending. He was hers and she was his.

"Yes, Dash! I'll marry you!"

And then they kissed. It was the fourth of July, Christmas Day, and her birthday all wrapped into one. The snow drifted and blew, carrying across their lips as they parted. Jaycee opened her mouth and stuck out her tongue to catch a flake. Life...life was good. It was dear and fragile and not to be tarried with.

Dash let out a yell.

Light spilled from the kitchen and out onto the pavement. Faces appeared in the doorway and Dash's smile widened. He grinned from ear to ear.

Pulling the little black box from his pocket, he opened it and placed the ring on Jaycee's right hand then snapped the box shut and rewarmed her with kisses on each and every finger.

Spring

CHAPTER ONE

"Momma, if wedding dresses weren't meant to be pink then why are there so many in this here store?" Jaycee's smile widened as she clutched the puffy blush dress covered from waist to hem with roses.

She couldn't contain her happiness. It seemed to spill over wherever she found herself. It was spring, with winter taking a back seat early in March and tulips and daffodils bursting on the scene. Her wedding was soon and she still didn't have a dress. She had plumb worn out her Daddy. This was the fifth dress shop in a fifty mile radius they had visited and he'd stopped coming after the second.

Dash's Aunt Katie and her Momma just smiled at her enthusiasm, undiminished despite the hundreds and hundreds of dresses they had looked at. They forgot, Jaycee loved to shop. Had gone through bridal magazines even as a child. And try as she might, it was hard to pick just one. The problem being now...it had to fit just so with little alteration because in a few short weeks, she would be Mrs. Dash Mattheson.

***

Jaycee pushed the notebook towards Dash for the third time. "I need yer help."

"And I'm willin', darlin', but it's your choice. It won't much matter to me."

She stamped her right foot in response and pulled the notebook from between the two of them. He willed his words back, but they were out there now. "You know what I mean. Whatever you want will be perfect."

"But I don't know what I want. I need yer help!" She sighed and ran a hand across her forehead.

Dash tentatively held out a hand. She looked down at his fingers, clearly irritated. Her eyes narrowed and she flipped the book back within his reach, releasing it as it touched the tips of his fingers. He grabbed and caught the white beribboned spiral book, gazing at the cover, "Bride's Planning Bible". *More like Bridezilla's.* He began to grin but squashed it, his eyes moving to Jaycee and he quickly opened the book, flipping through pages and pages of notes, sketches, pictures, and lists.

"That one there." She pointed. A yellow tab clung to the page edge labeled *Table Centerpieces.*

"So what are the choices?" he asked, the words all popping out of him at once. He sat down as he spoke, more of a fall into the relative safety of the brown tweed couch, praying for understanding. He tried to care, he really did...about the flowers, cake topper, color scheme. It was just dizzying the scope of detail over minutia.

Jaycee ticked off from memory, not stopping to breathe. "A round vase with glitter on the bottom half and real flowers. We could do that and include a candle. There's also the idea of tiny bottles in different sizes, maybe four or so on each table with a simple bud in each; again, a candle could be somewhere in the placement. And...well, look at the list and I've printed a few pictures." She paced back and forth then landed by the kitchen entrance, "Think about it. Envision each in yer head. I'll be right back."

Dash leaned forward, looking at the splashes of color before him. He flipped the page to view glued in pictures and the swipe of nail polish near one in particular. Jaycee's scrawl lay in between. *Pink Dove. Turquoise Stone. Alabaster Glitter.* He was beginning to see why people eloped to Vegas.

He closed his eyes and counted to three, plopping his finger onto the page. He opened his eyes just as quickly when he heard Jaycee closing a cabinet loudly in the kitchen and returning. She walked to his side and looked down at his haphazardly placed finger. Sliding onto the couch next to him, she took his other hand in hers, bringing it to her cheek. Her eyes became teary and she gave a tentative smile.

Dash relaxed. Crisis averted. He looked down at what he'd picked. Small wooden boxes with chipped paint and bunches of flowers peeking from within met his gaze. *Better'n a sharp stick in the eye.*

***

There it hung. Wrapped in a white garment bag, the oversized hanger peeked out and clung to the back of the closet door. The Dress. Steamed and fresh from the store. A perfect fit.

Jaycee sat cross-legged on her bed, her mind caving to the serenity of the blank white canvas and diving into the silence and oblivion. No lists called out from the notebook and magazines littering her space. Forgetting her phone and to-do's, peace stole over her. She imagined Dash's face when he saw her for the first time. Tears pricked her eyes and clung to her lashes. This was it. Grown up and married. To Dash! How did it happen so fast? Yet, she had waited a lifetime for it. For him, even when she'd found him the most annoying boy in Georgia.

She glanced away and back to the chaos around her. It was too much. How could she get it all organized, done and still *be the bride*?

A moment later, she heard a loud knock at the door and Kitty ducked her head in.

"You're here!" Jaycee exclaimed, jumping from the bed, causing a paper explosion. Ignoring the mess, she wrapped her arms around Kitty's neck in a tight squeeze.

"Geez Louise. Look at this place," Kitty responded with a loose hug then stepped back.

Jaycee's eyes swept the room then came to rest again on Kitty. She inspected her friend closely. "Did you just get in? You look...exhausted."

"Last night before dinner. And I am." She shrugged Jaycee's concern away and pushed a magazine towards the center of the bed to sit.

Jaycee bent to pick up the loose papers that had flown to the floor then resumed her position on the bed, facing the dress. Kitty followed her gaze.

"That it?"

"It is! Do you want to see?"

"Can't wait! I know you sent me a picture, but..."

Jaycee handed Kitty her bride's binder then went over to the closet door.

"Can you look at the list, see what the maid of honor wants to help with? Hint-Hint."

Kitty nodded and opened it as Jaycee dressed.

"Don't peek yet."

"I won't. This is fascinating reading by the way."

Jaycee laughed. "Stop, Kitty. This is serious."

Kitty looked up then to see Jaycee as she turned in the pink flowing concoction.

"Wow! Amazing! And so you."

Jaycee cocked an eyebrow. "So it's not too over the top?"

"Are you seriously worried about *that*?"

Jaycee looked down at the dress, lifting it slightly to display her toes. "No. I just wanted to hear what you thought. Do you love it?"

"I do and you're breathtaking. Dash will be mesmerized." Kitty stood and crossed the room to Jaycee, taking her hand. "I'm so happy for you."

"Thank you, sweets." Jaycee leaned in to hug Kitty, but she backed away. Jaycee frowned, noticing the worry in her friend's eyes. "Okay. Enough about me."

She shed the dress quickly, careful to hang it on the numerous hangers to keep it from wrinkling. "Your maid of honor dress is in the closet. You want to try it on?"

Kitty shook her head emphatically, biting her lower lip. Jaycee grabbed for her hand. "Hey, tell me what's goin' on."

Kitty's face crumpled. She seemed indecisive, turning from Jaycee and facing the bed. "I – I just can't. Oh!" Kitty said, burst into tears and running from the room.

Jaycee threw on the last of her clothes and quickly looked through the house for Kitty. Her car was still in the driveway. Finally she found her near the fence by the horses in the back corral. As she approached, Kitty let out a sigh and faced Jaycee.

"I'm okay. Sorry. I don't want to ruin this for you," she said, wiping the remnant of tears from her face.

"You're not." Jaycee drew closer and reached for her hand. "What is it? Your job, Todd, your mom?"

"You remember, Todd and I broke up four months ago. It's not him or any of that other stuff." She avoided Jaycee's eyes and kicked at a rock between the tufts of grass at her feet. Ginger, the 2-year-old mare approached them and whinnied softly which drew both of their gazes.

"Why does life have to be so confusing? Sometimes I think it'd be better to be born an animal with limited choices." Jaycee heard the catch in Kitty's voice, who had reached between the fence to pat the horse's soft muzzle.

Jaycee was silent as she listened to the sounds of midday settle over the farm. The birds sang with joy as they flew from tree to tree, gathering twigs and new green leaves for their nests. Cows lowed in the distance and a tractor could be heard far afield breaking up ground in anticipation of planting.

"When you're ready to talk, I'm here." Jaycee tilted her head, measuring her words, "You're not ruining anything. Life is fraught with problems and we can't always choose their timing, Kitty."

"It's my own fault."

"What?"

Kitty stood motionless, a grim expression on her face.

"Okay." Silence stretched as they both gazed at Ginger and the stud, Buster. "Our Ginger's expecting." No response except for the further drooping of Kitty's shoulders. "Hey, do you want to go with me to Dash's shop then get some lunch? Get yer mind off things?"

Kitty nodded. "Bring your book. I'll look at it on the way. Knowing you, there's lotsa glitter."

Jaycee smiled as she tugged Kitty from the fence and towards the back of the house. "Well, I am marrying Hot Flash Dash!"

***

He didn't always think clear when Jaycee was around. The anticipation of her arrival left Dash wandering around his office then straightening the papers on his desk. Two weeks now he'd be marrying the woman who eternally flustered, confounded, and drove him to distraction. Love was a funny thing. He sat suddenly, his right hand reaching for the computer mouse to continue working.

A knock fell on the closed door and he called out "Come on in".

It was Colt.

"What's going on, man?" Dash smiled. All was right in his world. An amazing woman, two hard working mechanics, a thriving business. And it just happened that he and Colt had become fast friends after hiring him the past winter.

"The Tucker van is all set. Just finished up."

"Great. Katie know?"

"She's calling them now. Thought I'd eat. You want something?"

Dash shook his head, lifting the cooler at his feet. "Jaycee and Kitty should be here soon. The maid of honor is back in town." Dash smiled suddenly, "Hey, I bet you and Kitty would hit it off!"

Colt looked down at his oil stained hands and service shirt. "Maybe we should hold off on introductions."

A whoosh of air sucked from the small office as the front door in the room beyond opened. Dash heard Jaycee's greeting to his aunt Katie. He grinned at Colt. "I don't think you have much of a choice now."

Colt swiped a hand through his hair and gave Dash a wry grin. "Why do I feel as if I've entered the lion's den?"

Jaycee bounded into the room, her smile contagious. Dash came around the desk and swept her into his arms. "The future Mrs. Matheson." Kissing her full on the mouth.

"As I live and breathe," Jaycee exclaimed after she caught her breath. "And in front of the children too." She said, winking. "How do, Colt? This is Kitty, my best friend and maid of honor."

Colt stepped forward and offered his hand to Kitty, who took it and bobbed her head at him. Dash noticed Jaycee's sidelong glance. Her thoughts seemed to mirror his own.

"I haveta ask you about something, wedding-related." Jaycee said, handing the manila envelope to Dash. "Nothing scary. We need to decide on the final menu for Harvey."

Harvey was the town caterer. While he didn't quit his day job, he made the best barbeque for hundreds of miles.

Dash grinned. "This should be a pleasant job." He withdrew the photocopied list from the envelope, scanning down the items and noting the prices and quantities. "Do you want to decide right now?" He raised his eyebrows as he looked from Jaycee to Kitty and Colt.

Kitty was nonplussed, tracing the outline of a screw on the back of a chair at the side of his desk.

Colt seemed to shake himself awake, having been following Kitty's movements with his eyes. "I'm goin' to grab a sandwich. You want one? How about you ladies?" Colt offered, as he made for the door.

"Another time perhaps. Kitty and I are goin' to Karl's. Can you spare some time, either of you?"

"We're backed up, but another time," Dash answered, the list still in his hands. "I'll look at this and we can talk tonight. Okay?"

She nodded, her eyes speaking volumes across the expanse where their two friends were concerned.

CHAPTER TWO

"I don't think I can, Jaycee." Kitty's dark head dipped as she studied the well-worn, lime green menu.

"You said yourself it's been ages since you and Todd broke up. Besides, I bet Colt Tanner can take yer mind off *any* problem." Jaycee thought back to the man's dark hair and rugged good looks. And she'd noticed that Kitty had cast more than one sidelong glance in his direction.

"Twain, Georgia was never in my long-term plans." Kitty's eyes teared up, then became round. "Course, I guess that remains to be seen."

"Whatdya' mean?" Jaycee pushed the menu aside, having memorized it from years working there.

"Just thinking it may be time to kiss New York goodbye."

"But you love it there and ... and the magazine!" Jaycee reached for Kitty across the table.

"I need to be practical." She thrust her chin forward meeting Jaycee's eyes.

Jaycee read fear there despite her brave pose. She wouldn't push her, but this was not the Kitty Jaycee knew. In all their years as friends, it was the first time she'd seen Kitty unsure of anything.

"We are goin' on a double date. It'll get yer mind from the work mess." Jaycee said, nodding then to Marlene, the waitress. "Do you know what you want? I'm famished!"

Marlene approached the table, asking Jaycee about the wedding which was quickly approaching. Jaycee'd invited nearly everyone in town. Karl had offered to make the cake free of charge, for which Jaycee was thankful. His talents as a pastry chef were well-known, but he only made cakes for friends.

Jaycee ordered an Ivan, thin sliced roast beef served with red onion, Swiss, and thousand island dressing grilled on pumpernickel.

"I'll have the same." Kitty said absently, glancing at the phone on the table by her elbow then towards the door to Karl's as it opened with the tinkling of the bell. "Hey, isn't that your friend Nancy?"

Jaycee looked up and into the face of a very harried Nancy Owens. "Can you excuse me for a sec?"

"Sure." She said, grabbing at her phone on the tabletop.

Jaycee pushed herself from the vinyl booth and met Nancy at the cash register. "Hey."

"Oh, I was just thinking of you! What a Godsend!" She blew a fringe of bangs from her face and exhaled a deep breath, grasping Jaycee's arm with one hand.

"What's goin' on?"

"We've been to Mercy Hospital with Rebecca. They wanted to fly her to Children's but we decided to drive her ourselves. That flight would scare her to death."

"What's the matter. Is she okay?"

"We ordered her favorite grilled cheese for the ride." Nancy's eyes met Marlene's over Jaycee's shoulder. She dropped her voice, but included Marlene in the conversation. "She's been dizzy and throwing up. They did an MRI in the ER and there's something there, Jaycee. Something on her brain."

"Oh my gosh." Jaycee's eyes filled with tears. "What – what can I do to help?"

Nancy took a set of keys from her purse and pushed them at Jaycee. "Can you close up the store tonight? Maybe help there for a few days, make sure the girls come in as scheduled and we're covered?"

"Yes, you know I can." Jaycee had filled in for a few people over the past few months when

Nancy'd needed the extra help. She'd also taught Jaycee how to make deposits, order stock, and call in hours to the payroll company. "Don't you worry. I can take care of all of it 'til you get back."

"I'll call you tonight, after closing time. Maybe we'll know more by then." Nancy leaned over and handed Marlene a ten dollar bill and took a brown bag from the counter. She walked towards the door, not waiting for her change.

"Be careful driving, Nancy." Jaycee called, rushing after her and giving her a quick hug.

Nancy's eyes filled. "Tom's driving. I can't — I'm just a mess right now. But we need to be strong for Rebecca."

Jaycee nodded and watched as she left the restaurant, following her movements out into the parking lot and getting into back of the gray minivan. She could see Rebecca's small head next to Nancy's as she slammed the door. Tom sped off quickly. Jaycee took a deep breath for all of them and silently prayed to God for the little girl.

***

Dash drove in the last nail in the new fence post and wiped a sleeve across his brow. He stood back to survey his work. Cattle lowed far afield and after giving a satisfied nod, Dash faced them, leaning forward onto the now sturdy section of fence. The cracked rotted piece discarded at his feet.

Since his aunt Katie held down the shop from 11 to 5 most days, Dash had taken to helping out on the Hamilton farm in the afternoons. It satisfied some part of Dash he hadn't known existed, to feel connected with the land and be a steward over it.

Having grown up around farming families, it'd always been a yearning within him, even older than his love for fixing cars, a dream that had somehow died after his injuries in the fire. It'd been replaced with fantasies of a life with Jaycee and now that life was within reach. A wife, family, a home...these were all part of it.

Dash looked at his hands, the calluses having become toughened over the weeks working outside, a different sort of dirty than working in the shop. Was this in God's plan for his life, when just a year ago it'd just been him and Casper, his trusty cat?

He saw his newest sidekick then run alongside the outside of the fence. Marcus. The boy had taken to coming home, doing his homework, and taking off outside to find Dash. He knew it'd renewed Jeb Hamilton's faith that his son would someday want to take over the farm, especially now that he was limited in what he could do with his stability slowly decreasing. Jeb now used the cane that he'd once given Dash and his speech had taken on a slower quality.

"Dash!"

"Hey, boy. You ready to work?" Dash bent and gathered the discarded wood at his feet. He motioned to the tools on the ground. "Grab those, will ya?"

Marcus nodded, quick to take up the container of nails, hand saw, and hammer. "Where we headed?"

"Shed to put these away then we'll check in with Clyde." They walked side by side over a crest in the land and towards the corral. "How was school?"

"Same boring math, science, and English." Marcus made a face which Dash caught out of the corner of his eye.

"I never was one for the books either, but you just keep at it so you can graduate."

"Yeah. I know. I'm not goin' to college though." Marcus bent his head, his eyes on his feet as they traversed the ruts in the land, keeping the tools steady.

"No? I pegged you as a college man. Computers, maybe?" Dash fished.

"Naw. That's just for games. I'll be here. Helpin' momma on the farm, as daddy's always wanted."

Dash stopped, which in turn caused Marcus to pause in his concentration on his feet and look up. "What?"

"I'm real proud of you. For stepping up." He clapped the boy on his back. "Have you told your parents your decision?"

"I expect they'll figure it out," he said, shrugging.

"I expect so," Dash said, laughing.

They continued walking. Before entering the large shed off to the right of the barn, Dash deposited the scrap wood on top of the wood pile. The shed was really a large barn itself, housing the farming tools along with bigger equipment for mowing and plowing, and feed for the animals.

Clyde was there sharpening the blades of a large pair of pruning shears. He paused as he worked, acknowledging the two of them with a gruff "Hello".

Marcus put the tools back in their proper spots while Dash approached the older man.

"Wood's replaced. Anything you need doin', Marcus and I are game."

Clyde peered out the open shed door, squinting at the angle of the sun. "Horses need feed and fresh water."

Dash knew this was Marcus' favorite job. The old man winked at him as he looked at the boy, who was returning the saw to a nail on the wall.

"Let's go, Marcus! Yer sister will be here soon enough and I gotta get my afternoon kisses in." Dash half-teased. This was his favorite part of the day, seeing Jaycee at the Hamilton home and spending time on the back porch holding her hand.

"Yuck," Marcus said loudly, then squirmed out of the way of Dash's hand meant to ruffle the boy's hair. He grabbed a bucket by the shed door and slid past the shed doors out into the afternoon sunshine.

***

Dash was sitting on the back porch with Marcus when Jaycee arrived home. Kitty had bowed out, claiming the need for a nap. Worry over her and Rebecca had made Jaycee wipe tears off her cheeks several times on the way home from Karl's.

She left the bridal binder in her car, her heart hesitant to plan a celebration right now. With Daddy's health slowly declining, she'd been forcing herself to think on the wedding and all the details to push off the worry. Now she was just exhausted herself. She flopped down into the chair next to Dash. He looked across at her as she let out a deep sigh. He grabbed her hand and leaned forward.

In one swift movement, Marcus said 'hi and bye', bursting from the screened porch and out onto the back lawn running towards the horses in their corral, one hand stuffed in his pocket.

"Sugar cubes?" Jaycee asked, slight amusement breaking her somber mood.

"Yeah, he couldn't take it anymore. Plus I told him I was waitin' to kiss my soon-to-be bride."

"Dash, I – " Her voiced still him. "Maybe we shouldn't."

"Shouldn't what? Kiss?" He stood before her then and swept her up into his arms, cradling her against him. "Woman, you best get used to this." He bent his head and closed his eyes, his lips whispering promises as they met hers. She melted against him, responding to his comfort and thanking God for his strength, willing it into her own body.

Once his lips released hers, he sat back down in the chair with Jaycee still in his arms. She laid her head on his chest. She was ready to give up, be in the here and now and not think about anything. But she couldn't.

She lifted her head. "I don't know if we can...be happy with so much pain."

"Pain?" Dash's brow furrowed.

"Daddy getting worse. Kitty...something's very wrong and she won't tell me what." She shook her head.

"Thinkin' Colt may be the solution there."

"Maybe. I'm not real sure. I think they'd be great together too, but there's more..."

"There'll always be pain, Jaycee." He sat up straighter and Jaycee tilted her chin looking him in the face. "We can't let it stop us from living."

"But now – Nancy's Rebecca...she's real sick, Dash." She blinked her eyes rapidly. "They've taken her to Children's. There's something on her brain."

She saw his face drain of color and concern come into his dark green eyes. "What can we do?"

"I'm closing the store tonight and helping with that for a while." Jaycee bit her lip. "Prayer, I expect right now is all we can do."

"Then let's get to it." Dash went to bow his head, but then raised his eyes to Jaycee's. "No more talk of postponing things. We'll take on life's sorrows and joy's together. We can't let it deter the future, Jaycee."

She nodded, still unsure but bowed her head to join her prayers to Dash's softly spoken ones.

***

Kitty didn't know if she could do it. Tell Jaycee or anyone, but she was past the point of no return, wasn't she? In the privacy of her bedroom, her hands flew to her stomach as she rested on her bed. Tiny movements stretched her taut stomach. She'd be going on four months if her calculations were right. The tiny life all her friends had told her to snuff out. She just couldn't.

She'd made the mistake of confiding in two of her friends at the magazine and the news had spread like wildfire. Kitty had left after that. She'd given away most of her things, paid up her lease 'til the end, and let her roommate know she'd be moving back home.

But was it what she wanted? Was this the best course? What were her options now? To have the baby and keep it. She couldn't give it up for adoption. No one here in Twain knew but how long would it be until she started showing?

Tears stung her eyes as she curled onto her side and cradled her stomach. The baby pushed and fluttered against her hand. She should be thinking about Jaycee's shower tomorrow and her part in the wedding, not herself right now. Her cell phone buzzed near her hand on the bed. She looked at the text message.

Closing for Nancy at 9. Want to hit a movie?

Kitty typed back. *I'm tired.*

Come on! It will do your soul good. I've missed you.

Kitty considered. She could nap now and wake up later, hopefully more refreshed. It would be nice to be with Jaycee, who had a firm head on her shoulders and hold on her beliefs. Kitty's faith had tilted so much since she'd moved away, like a teeter totter.

Okay.

Great, we'll pick you up a bit after 9.

We'll? Maybe Dash was coming? Or maybe...oh no. Kitty couldn't see herself on a date right now.

Who's we? She typed back, holding her breath until she saw Jaycee's answer then expelled it all at once.

The guys and us...you, me, Dash, and Colt. It will be fun and NO pressure.

Great. Four months pregnant and being set up on a date. Too tired to respond, Kitty dropped the phone back on the bed and closed her eyes.

CHAPTER THREE

A chick-flick won out over the three other movies showing at the small theatre. Dash had taken Jaycee over to the mall and hung out with her as she closed *Heaven Sent* then they'd picked up Colt and Kitty, respectively. Jaycee had picked the movie online and they were in their seats with popcorn in hand for it to start at 9:35.

They were seated Dash – Jaycee – Kitty – Colt, arranged he was sure with some forethought by Jaycee. Their two friends weren't dumb. They knew this was a setup. Kitty'd been looking tired and drawn, not her usual bubbly self. But Colt was reliable and steady, like a constant stream through the crags of the foothills and Dash expected that was just what Kitty needed right now.

He put his arm around Jaycee and she leaned her head briefly on his shoulder. The theatre darkened and the movie began. Their fingers met in the popcorn container and he smiled to himself in the darkness.

He leaned down and whispered, "Quit stealing my kernels."

"Get used to it." He could hear the grin in her voice. He saw her move again towards the bowl in her lap and his hand met hers, purposely this time. His brain screamed at him to lift her fingers to his mouth, wanting to taste the buttery saltiness against her flesh. But he refrained, pushing the thought away and briefly squeezing her hand.

She turned her head towards him. Her eyes burned into his, desire mirroring his own. Fourteen more days now.

He concentrated on the screen before him, the movie's opening credits beginning to scroll through. An hour later, Dash found himself laughing at the romantic escapades on the screen. It was the classic plotline: girl meets boy, girl loses boy, girl gets boy back. There were a few funny scenes. He'd looked over at Colt and Kitty during the movie. They were laughing and he saw Colt lean in to talk to Kitty several times. Apparently, he thought Kitty was something special after all.

***

Jaycee's phone was blowing up. Texts from her Momma, Kitty, Dash, even Marcus! She'd opened the store an hour before, making sure Clara and Lisa had shown for their shifts. Midday, Tina was expected then two more girls would show for the night shift. She'd posted her cell number in the back for emergencies then given a quick perusal of inventory and back stock. Nancy'd been in touch with her briefly the night before, making sure things were fine, but having no further news on Rebecca.

Jaycee flew another prayer up to heaven. She couldn't imagine the worries going through Tom and Nancy's minds right now. *Dear God, give*

them Your strength and peace. Please give the
doctors wisdom and help heal Rebecca. Amen.

Jaycee pulled her red Chrysler LeBaron into
the *Fast Lane's Bowling* parking lot then tilted the
mirror to look at her hair, tucking a stray piece of
her long blonde bangs behind her ear. She was
supposed to meet Kitty and her momma to go over
the last minute details for the wedding and make a
schedule of how to complete the remaining
decorations in time. She hoped Kitty was feeling
better today.

Jaycee jumped from the car with her
wedding organizer and into the unusually warm
day, her skin singing in contact with the fragrant
morning air. Jaycee'd chosen a light purple
sundress with a cream cropped sweater for the
day. As she entered the double doors of the
bowling alley, a breeze kicked up and she caught
the smell of the bright orange begonias in the
flower beds. She loved spring.

She absently looked at her phone one last time before placing it back into her bag. She was surprised when she looked up and saw her father and Dash standing near the front counter.

"Well now. Shouldn't you two be busyin' yerselves with something? Didn't know our little meeting included the two favorite men in my life." Jaycee joked, coming up beside Dash. He slipped a hand around her back and pulled her close to kiss her quickly on the cheek.

Jaycee's Momma appeared just then with Kitty in tow. "Now, darlin'. Come with us." She took Jaycee by the hand and led her towards the side of the bowling alley and down a long corridor. Throwing open the doorway at the end of the hall, she pulled Jaycee forward.

"Momma!" Jaycee said, laughing at her mother's insistence and glancing back towards Kitty who took the bridal book from between Jaycee's hands. Just as she went to protest, she heard a loud "Surprise!" shouted in a cacophony of voices.

Jaycee whipped her head back around to see friends and family gathered in the large function room. A "Congratulations" sign hung between the floor to ceiling length windows. To the left of the door, chafing dishes and covered casseroles stood at the ready on long tables along with paper plates and cups, two punch bowls, and a huge iced white cake.

Moments later, Dash joined her side as people surged forward to kiss and hug the couple. Old Mrs. Owens was there along with Donna, her great granddaughter. Eileen Casey and her family shook their hands, along with Cora and Mike Tubbins with their baby and twin sons.

She blinked back tears. This was Jaycee's bridal shower! She'd been so busy worrying about the details of the wedding that she'd forgotten one of the timeworn traditions.

A few minutes later, Dash and Jaycee were led to a table in the center of the room where Jaycee sat down. Other tables formed a big square around it with more tables against the walls. People mingled and laughter rang throughout the room. Jaycee saw her Momma grab her father's cane-free hand and lead him to stand nearby.

"Your attention, please. We'd like to welcome you to Jaycee and Dash's shower. We're glad you came to celebrate with us." Applause and shouts of approval drowned out her Daddy's voice, but then things quieted down as he held up a hand. Jaycee saw her Momma poke him in the ribs with her elbow.

He cleared his throat and continued on as people shuffled to sit down and others stood in small groups. Marcus came to stand next to his Daddy. He encircled the boy with one arm. "Before we get started on the food I'd like to give Jaycee and Dash a little something then say grace."

Jaycee's momma produced a long white envelope from her bag.

"We love Dash like a son and wish them all the happiness in the world. This here — . "

Jaycee's mother waved the envelope and then stepped in behind her husband to hand it to Dash, who had remained standing.

"Is the deed to 20 acres of land next to our own." Lifting the cane, he swiped at one eye with the back of his hand.

Jaycee looked from her father to Dash's face. His eyes had gone wide and he opened his mouth several times to say something. He looked down at Jaycee and she smiled up into his face. She stood and reached up to kiss his cheek then nodded. He made his way around the table and caught Marcus up under his arms and swung him around, giving a whoop.

Depositing him back on the ground, he hugged her Daddy, thanking him heartily and then embraced her Momma. Jaycee knew Dash's love of the land had been growing. As they sat on the back porch in the afternoon's slanted light, he'd cross his scuffed cowboy boots at the ankle and tell her of his work on the farm that day. It was as if the land was singing and weaving a pattern of its own over the fabric of his life, but he'd just discovered its song.

Not much later, the whole party had eaten their fill of the potluck dishes, cold cut plate, salads, and appetizers. The middle table was exchanged for the gift table, Clint Sparrow and his son Todd hoisting the overladen rectangle and showing their brawn.

A chair was produced for Jaycee and she settled into it with Dash watching from the sidelines. Kitty was at her right side keeping track of what gifts were from who. Marcus helped by grabbing the crumpled papers as they fell to the floor and discarding them into a trash bag.

By the end of the gift opening, Jaycee and Dash were the proud owners of two blenders, three sets of dishes, new utensils for the kitchen, bath towels, a kitchen clock, a microwave from Aunt Katie, and various and sundry items too numerous to count.

One in particular had made Jaycee blush red to the roots of her hair and she'd quickly shoved it back into the little pink bag with a smile and embarrassed "thank you". The older women raised their eyebrows and the younger ones laughed loudly. As the party wound down and the last gift was opened, Jaycee's momma presented her with a keepsake bonnet festooned with bows and ribbons.

Jaycee posed for more pictures then turned to Dash at her side. With tears in her eyes, she grabbed his arm and pulled him close. The world faded away, the noise of kids running, parents wrangling, others cleaning up now just background noise to the rush of intimacy with him. He tipped her face up with his hand gentle on her chin.

"Is it really okay to be so happy? I'm afraid the other shoes about to drop. It's danglin' over my head."

"The ribbons and the memories, they'll protect you. God's got you and so do I." He wrapped his arms around her and hugged her tightly. She turned her head and rested her cheek against his chest, closing her eyes then opening them briefly. She met Kitty's gaze from across the room and saw an indescribable sadness there. Jaycee blinked back tears and tried to smile at her friend. *What on earth could be wrong?*

***

Kitty wanted to run away from her worries and just be...*Kitty*. She missed who she was, before all the fears and unknowns had appeared. It's not like she had anyone to blame but herself. But right now, she wanted to not care and return to being the fashionable, up and coming editor for *Acclaim*

Magazine. Yet, here she was back in Twain, Georgia living with her mother.

Colt had texted her earlier in the afternoon, mid-party. She'd slipped her phone out and stared at his words. He seemed like a nice guy. Sweet as yesterday's iced tea and her type, tall, dark and handsome. They'd talked some at the movies and in the car on the way home. He had a small apartment, worked for Dash, and was into rock climbing and canoeing in his spare time. Out-doorsy, well...one strike on the Kitty type. Not that she didn't like the outdoors, she'd just been in the city for so many years, it hadn't been a priority in a long time.

Nightlife, parties, late night sessions with the marketing team as a new monthly issue was about to be released, mingling for business and pleasure. That was the world Kitty could relate to. But seeing Dash and Jaycee's relationship, she found a new tug on her heart. The one for a steady guy and a family. But the order in that equation was messed up. She'd done it backwards.

Back in her room, she put the TV on for noise and sat on her bed. She knew she'd be showing soon. It was a miracle she wasn't already. Naked it was obvious, but dressed in baggy clothes, she'd hidden her condition. For how long? She'd have to tell her mother and then her grandmother and aunts would all come to gather and give their opinions.

Kitty scrolled through the apps on her phone, scrolling her way back into Messages. Why not? She ignored the gentle pressure against her bladder and shifted slightly, her fingers hanging over the illuminated letters.

Sorry, I was gone most of the day. She bit her lip. Would he be around?

Her phone lit up a few minutes later. *Hey! Was just thinking about you.*

Really? Kitty stretched her legs before her and settled into the pillow at her back. This could get interesting. She thought back to the moment her eyes locked with Jaycee's that afternoon. It wasn't fair. Kitty wanted the happily ever after too. Was it even possible anymore?

CHAPTER FOUR

Jaycee had spent the last two days organizing the stacks of gifts that had overtaken the dining room. She'd shuttled numerous things to Dash's apartment, where they'd be living after the wedding. Now she cleared the last large box off the table at her parent's house and plopped several bags of craft supplies onto the middle.

Kitty would be there soon and she and Jaycee were putting together the centerpieces today. Jaycee had painted the miniature crate-type boxes white. The paint was now dry and they'd sand it in spots to look shabby chic then add the silk flowers Jaycee had found on clearance. They needed 22 centerpieces for the tables.

She pulled the hot glue sticks free of a bag along with a glue gun. One of them could work on sanding while the other glued in the flowers. It shouldn't take them long. She heard the doorbell ring and ran to the front hall. Kitty stood there looking more relaxed than she had the other day. She'd been checking in with her, but her vague answers had Jaycee wondering.

"Hey! Just gettin' the supplies out. Come on in." Jaycee led the way to the dining room.

Kitty followed and sniffed appreciatively. "What's that smell?"

"Momma's made us some munchies. Macaroons and buffalo chicken dip."

"God's honest truth," she said in typical Kitty fashion, "it's about makin' me swoon."

Laughing, Jaycee took her hand and led her into the kitchen. "And it's makin' the southern come out in you too. Let's eat first!"

The crockpot was making little popping sounds on the countertop. She pulled open a cabinet and took out the corn chips, dumping them into a bowl while Kitty took a seat at the island. Jaycee put those before Kitty then scooped some of the hot dip into a serving dish with a spoon. She flipped the crockpot temperature gauge to warm then slid into the stool next to Kitty.

They both munched in silence for several minutes, the crunch of the chips loud in the quiet house.

"Where is everyone?" Kitty asked between bites.

"Marcus is at school and Daddy 's out back. Momma's shopping with Aunt Katie. Gettin' the chalk board to write on and direct people towards the peach grove and some Sharpies to write on those flat river rocks I bought."

"I saw that in your binder. Great idea to have marriage advice from guests written on those."

"Looks like we're almost done. Last thing is for you to try on your dress. Today, Kitty." Jaycee gave her a look as she licked some dip from her fingers. "After we eat."

Kitty blinked rapidly and cleared her throat. "Guess it's been put off long enough."

She stood then and wandered towards the sink, washing her hands then drying them on the towel hanging at the front of the stove.

"Do you mind if I take a few?" Kitty eyed the white mountain of fluffy macaroons on the countertop.

"Sure enough and bring me two, will ya?" Jaycee let out a groan. "We'll be lucky if either of us fit into our dresses."

Her mouth full and walking back to stand by Jaycee, Kitty tilted her head to the side and handed Jaycee the cookies. She gulped down her food and opened her mouth to speak. Nothing came out. She walked to the refrigerator near the back door. "You want a drink?"

"Yes, please." Jaycee ate the macaroons in two bites. They melted in her mouth. "Milk."

Kitty nodded and poured them both a cup and went to sit back next to Jaycee. She took a small sip and put her glass down with some finality.

Jaycee looked up in surprise, her hands at her stomach for all she'd eaten.

"I've got something important to tell you."

Jaycee waited. The hum of the appliances causing a rhythm in the room she'd previously been unaware of. This was it. She prayed silently for Kitty. Whatever it was had taken a lot of courage for her to talk about. She grabbed for Kitty's hand and they sat there with the remnants of their snack before them.

"I – I'm pregnant, Jaycee." Silent tears slid down Kitty's face.

Jaycee tried to remain calm, but she couldn't help but glance at Kitty's stomach. Kitty nodded at her look. "Oh my gosh! Are you okay? Does your mother know? How about the father? Is the baby Todd's?"

The questions flew from Jaycee's mouth before she could clamp down on her tongue. She stood suddenly. "Come on, let's go into my room."

"But – but the decorations." Kitty stammered as she followed Jaycee past the dining room and into the familiarity of the bedroom.

"They'll wait. Sit."

"No. I need to show you." Kitty lifted her shirt. Large tears flowed down her cheeks and great sobs wrenched from her throat.

Jaycee could imagine how shocked her face looked. Kitty's stomach was, well...pregnant. Her belly button was still an inny but not for long. Her skin was taught across the little round bundle.

"Oh, Kitty. Why didn't you tell me before?"

"I couldn't. I told a few friends and it spread like wildfire at work. I've left. I'm done with New York. Now I – I'm here and...I don't know what to do."

She fell into Jaycee's arms. Jaycee stepped back and they both sat on the bed while Kitty cried.

"Well, what's there to do?" Commiserating at this point would only prolong the pain. Jaycee pulled Kitty away to look into her tear-stained face,

278

her eyes filling. "You're gonna have a baby and we best get to celebratin'." *Kitty with a baby. Well, don't that beat all.*

* * *

Jaycee didn't like to keep secrets from Dash but she also hadn't asked Kitty's permission to tell him. She said she'd need more time to tell her mother before news spread, which it was sure to. Kitty's dress for the wedding was snug, but Jaycee planned to ask her Momma to take it out an inch on each side, which would give her room to breathe.

A baby! Not only would she encourage Kitty to celebrate the new life growing within her, but also to not be ashamed. Sure, she'd made a mistake, but now she'd move forward and be the best mother she could. As the afternoon wore on, talk of what she would do had turned to forming a plan to find an OBGYN and starting prenatal vitamins.

Kitty had mentioned that she and Colt had been talking, both by text and in person. It seems he'd taken her for ice cream the other night. And again, they were going to dinner that evening. How would that fit into the picture? Surely Colt would need to know soon.

Jaycee drove home from the shopping mall. It was late. She'd stayed to go over the time cards, call in hours to payroll, and order some inventory for the small boutique. Her phone rang suddenly from the console between the two front seats.

"Hello?"

"Jaycee, it's Nancy."

"How are you? I'm just leavin' the store."

"Things okay there?"

"Yes, just fine. No problems. How's Rebecca." She held her breath as she turned down a long road connecting Lincoln with Twain, slowing the car as she concentrated on Nancy's words.

"They believe it's a benign tumor growing on Rebecca's pituitary gland. They're releasing us with some medicines to try and shrink it. We'll be home tomorrow afternoon!"

Jaycee let out a whoop. "Praise the Lord!"

"We've been rejoicing too!" Jaycee could hear the relief in her voice. "Rebecca's asleep. Tom and I are going to the cafeteria for a break. We're sagging with relief. We just — just can't thank you enough for the help with the store."

"My pleasure. So glad I could do somethin'. Payroll's set and I ordered a few things that were low in stock from the supplier catalog using the account." It was good to talk shop. She knew Nancy had had a rough couple of days. Jaycee used the next few minutes to catch her up on the store then they hung up with a promise Jaycee'd meet Nancy the next night at closing to go over some details and return her keys.

Tomorrow would come soon enough. Jaycee still wasn't a morning person, but Dash had said he had a surprise for her and he'd be at her house bright and early...a half-hour before sunrise.

***

Sleep clung to her eyes, yet she dug higher to consciousness, shaking the dream state from her head as she sat up. *Ting – Ting*. It couldn't be. Jaycee rushed to the window, glancing at her clock. Her alarm was due to go off in about ten minutes. Yet, there stood Dash. She pinched herself to make sure it wasn't one of her fondest memories resurfacing. She jumped from the sting, realizing as she did that it was the making of a new memory.

Dash had a flashlight and waved to her, the light swinging in the semi-darkness. He had a big grin on his face and motioned for her to come outside. She nodded and held up a hand to him. Throwing on a pair of jeans and a sweatshirt, she slid her feet into her Ugg boots and made her way outside.

"Boy, woman. Yer gettin' that time down on meetin' me in the yard." He opened the passenger side door to his truck.

"I'd say. You goin' to do this my whole life?" She smiled softly at him, looking up into his face as the sky lightened slightly.

He paused mid door slam and put his face close to hers. "I expect we'll be seein' our fair share of sunrises together." He kissed her lips and gently tugged on a length of hair by her ear. "Speaking of which," he straightened, "we're goin' to miss it if we don't get movin'.

Dash pulled the car out of the Hamilton's driveway then took a turn down Rickett Lane.

"Where we headed?" Jaycee asked.

"Our land," he said in hushed reverence, searching for Jaycee's hand across the seat. She slid closer and he put his arm around her as he drove. "There's a turn here, just a little dirt road. We can get in it a ways then it's a short walk."

Jaycee nodded, anticipation making her heart beat loudly in her ears. Within a few moments they'd arrived. Dash grabbed a blanket from the bed of the truck then clasped Jaycee's hand. They followed the path which got significantly narrower then widened some 300 feet in. There was a clearing as wide as half a football field before them.

"Wow," Jaycee breathed out.

"I've come here a few times, walking the land. It's beautiful, Jaycee. What do you think?"

"I can't believe it's ours."

Dash spread the blanket on the ground and swooped Jaycee up into his arms, spinning her around. She threw back her head, tilting it up towards the sky and closing her eyes. He stopped suddenly and bent forward to kiss her neck. It was dizzying, Dash and the early morning smells of the trees and grass around them.

He placed her on the blanket gently and lay next to her. The sky above them clung to the remnants of night. The glow of the sun began to show its face. They stilled in anticipation, their shoulders touching .

"Are you sure you want to settle here?" Dash asked quietly.

"It's home." Jaycee said, turning her face towards him.

"But your dreams." He said, not altering his gaze.

Jaycee sat up. "Were like the early stages of a pussy willow."

Dash looked at her then, a smile at the corners of his mouth. "A what?"

"A pussy willow. That soft gray fur on the outside, that's just the beginning of a long process in their growth. They bloom then the seeds come out and are blown away on the wind." Jaycee paused, her gaze on the tree line before them. "I expect the dreams I had were all fluff. The wonderings of a girl who knew nothing of the world. "

"And now you do?"

She nodded and faced him as he slowly sat up. "Dash, my dreams now are more substantial. The fluff has gone and fallen off and I'm all pollen and seeds, ready to put down roots and grow. This life matters. It's us and looking after Momma and Daddy as they age." She stood and moved forward, standing in the center of the open area. "Our children will roam this land, ride horses, go to the same schools we did. See that tree over there. It's old. Does it wish it was a banister or a boat sailing the seas? No, it's set its roots and they grow deep. They've been watered by God's hand Himself. It's content. As am I. I'll follow God's path before me here, even if it's only a few steps at a time."

CHAPTER FIVE

Dash entered his living room from the bedroom, straightening his shirt tails to tuck them in. Marcus stood in the center of the room, fooling with the tie at his neck.

"Here, let me help." Dash moved in front of the young man, turning the black tie at his neck into a neat cravat. "Whoo-wee, yer Momma is gonna be pleased as punch to see you dressed up like this." He took a walk around the young man.

Marcus strutted barefoot across the room in the black tux.

Dash grinned widely. "I think the effect may be better with shoes."

"Sure enough," Marcus said, sitting on the couch to examine the black socks and shoes from the rental store. Casper jumped up beside him wanting his ears scratched. Marcus complied, forgetting what he was about.

"Casper, you are a nudge." Dash scolded, sitting himself next to the two of them on the couch and rubbing the cats black belly as he flopped between them. "Glad I bought one of those lint brushes."

Out of the bathroom strolled Jeb, Jaycee's father.

"Hello, sir. You look dapper," Dash called out.

Jeb nodded, twirling his cane for effect. "Like three penguins going to an igloo open house."

The three of them laughed. Dash lost himself in thought, looking at Casper. "Gonna bring that momma home like I said I would, fella."

His eyes misted up, thinking back to the fire at his house and losing all of the tangible memories of his parents. He was glad Casper had made it out and that God had given them both another chance. He swallowed over the lump in his throat. His own mother and father sure would have loved Jaycee and her family.

"It'll be official soon," Jeb said, sitting in a nearby chair. "And if I don't get you two to the church on time, I'm in a heap of trouble."

"Except it's the peach orchard." They'd spent the day before setting up tables and chairs and the arch for the ceremony behind the Hamilton's home. "No better place in the world."

Jeb nodded, a grin on his face. "And God's seen fit to give us perfect weather. No need to use those tents."

Butterflies hit Dash's stomach, suddenly wondering how Jaycee was feeling at this very moment. It wouldn't be long now and they would be man and wife.

* * *

It must be a dream. Jaycee slid into the strapless light pink wedding gown. Her momma went around her and fluffed at the roses on the length of skirt as Kitty hooked and zipped the back. When they were finished, they both stood back. Jaycee looked from one to the other, unshed tears glistening in their eyes.

"Now, don't you go makin' me cry," she said tearily, her voice squeaking from her throat. She twirled in the dress, catching a vision of herself in the full length mirror in the corner. She heard the snap and pop of the camera. Tanya Cordley was their photographer for the day. She'd been taking shots since Jaycee had rolled out of bed at o-dark-thirty.

She started instructing them, asking for postures and poses. Jaycee's momma handed her a pair of round rhinestone earrings which she put on in front of the mirror. Kitty slid the rhinestone bracelet onto her wrist.

"It's about that time," Tanya stated, looking at her watch. "I'll go see if the groom has arrived."

"I best get out there," Jaycee's momma exclaimed. "Make sure yer uncles are doing their jobs directing everyone on where to park and how to get to the orchard around back."

She hustled from the room after Tanya. Jaycee's eyes flew about the room as they left. The night before had been her last under her parent's roof. The last night in her bed. She suddenly wondered if Dash slept in socks or snored. *Wow.* She should have asked these questions days...months ago. Did he move his leg back and forth like she did to get to sleep? Would that bother him? *Too late now, Hot Flash. Yer almost mine.*

Jaycee hugged her arms across her middle, tears tugging at her lashes. She refused them, blinking rapidly.

"Hey, you okay?" Kitty asked, quiet up until then. She came up beside Jaycee and pulled her into a gentle hug.

Jaycee sniffed. "All the yammerin' I did at Dash about the wedding. I've been fussin' and worryin' and I should have been enjoying our days." She shook her head regretfully.

"It's a bride thing, honey. I'm sure he understands."

"So many memories," Jaycee said, remembering sleepovers with Kitty with kitchen raids at midnight and stealing out to ride the horses in the moonlight in their pajamas. "I'm not a little girl anymore."

"You sure aren't." Kitty said tilting her head in concentration, fingering Jaycee's dress. "You're the sugar plum fairy."

Jaycee let out a whoop, reaching behind her to grab a pillow and aim it at Kitty's head.

***

The pink blossoms on the peach trees hung fragrant in the air, blowing gentle in the cool spring breeze. The guests had arrived and were on white chairs flanking an aisle created from their configuration and decorated with the spring grasses and dusted with white rose petals.

Kitty walked down the aisle on Marcus' arm to the accompaniment of a piano tucked between two trees atop a fabric covered piece of thick plywood. She stood to the side of the archway, her gaze extending to the right, out over the aquamarine linen covered tables standing off to the right of the ceremony area. The caterer had made himself scarce, encamping in Jaycee's momma's kitchen with last minute food prep.

Turning her head, Kitty couldn't help but seek out Colt's face in the crowd. He'd been there the day before to help Dash and the Hamilton's set up . The guests spilled to the left and right of the aisle and behind the chairs, too many for the seating available. Grandparents, parents, aunts, uncles, and friends came with kids in tow who were in fancy dress and being hushed in anticipation of the bride's arrival.

She found Colt standing off to the side. Her heart squeezed. He was so handsome, wearing a charcoal gray suit with crisp white shirt and matching dove-colored tie. He could surely rival any man in New York. He nodded at her, a slow grin coming onto his face. Her cheeks warmed under his gaze and she looked down at her knee length white dress. *The irony.* Kitty's countenance collapsed.

At that moment, the breeze blew and caught the fabric, pressing it against her swollen stomach. She looked up to see Colt's face, his eyes widening. *The messes you get yourself in, Kitty.* It looked like she'd be having a conversation with him sooner than tomorrow when she'd planned.

***

"And now, Dash and Jaycee would like to say a few words to one another."

A hush fell over the crowd. Dash's gaze fell from Jaycee's eyes to the ring in his right hand. He grasped her shaking left hand with his own. He cleared his throat nervously.

"I've loved you since I can remember. God has blessed me with the sunshine that is Jaycee Cozetta Hamilton. I promise to care for you, love you, and protect you all the days of my life. May God bless our marriage." He slid the gold and platinum band onto her finger, blinking back tears as she began to speak.

"Dash, you're my knight in shining armor, but better still because you're real. You've wooed me with fried chicken," she paused here to laugh softly, "and with your kind heart, intelligent mind, careful wit without injury, and love that can't compare. May God bless our marriage. I promise to love, honor, and keep you all the days of our lives."

Jaycee's slid the match to her own ring onto Dash's finger.

"Now by the authority given to me by the state of Georgia and by Almighty God, as his servant, I now pronounce you man and wife. You may kiss the bride."

His world became smaller, mere inches from him was everything he cared about. The love of his life, the woman he treasured above everything but the good Lord Himself. He let out a shout and drew Jaycee gently to him. His lips met hers with firm urgency. He pressed her body to him, clasping his arms around her in a warm hug. She responded, kissing him in glee. Triumphant and grinning, they parted and turned to face the residents of Twain, Georgia who were clapping and cheering, ready to join in with the celebration.

EPILOGUE

Jaycee placed her phone in the holder on the counter and turned on the wireless speaker. The smooth tones of Sarah McLachlan drifted on the air across the kitchen. On bare feet, she hurried over to the oven door, turning on the light to check the lasagna. Twenty minutes more and it would be perfection. She'd let it rest while she popped in the bread and finished the salad.

Dash was expected in from building a fence on the north side of their land, hopefully in enough time to shower before dinner. Jaycee heard a bang at the back door and peeked out. Bella had gotten free again and was butting her head against the screen door. Maybe she liked the music?

Jaycee grabbed a salt lick from the kitchen cabinet and squeezed outside through a small space in the door as she opened it. From experience, she knew it was near impossible to get a sheep out of the house once it found its way in.

They caused havoc, knocking things over and scaring themselves half to death.

She urged Bella forward holding the salt lick aloft, not affording her a taste until she neared the sheep pen. She peered around their pen, all tucked in for the night as they were, to see a gap the sheep must've squeezed through. *Another repair.* She opened the latch and led the wayward sheep back inside. She took one of the twist ties she kept tied high on the pen and secured the salt lick low for them to feast on.

"There ya go, Bella. Don't be thinkin' I'm gonna reward your wandering again." She patted the sheep's wool gently. The melody from the music wound its way out the screen door and into the back yard. Jaycee hummed the tune to the sheep as she checked on them one by one. There were five altogether. She was anticipating getting a ram a month from now. They'd have milk aplenty then to drink and extra to make cheeses. Just in time too.

Jaycee forgot herself, wandering over to the barn and pulling out the pliers. She returned to the pen to twist the metal back into shape. Sticking them into her jeans back pocket, she ran back into the house to finish dinner.

Dash must've gone in through the front door, for Jaycee heard the shower running over the music. She finished the salad and slid the bread into the oven. She washed her hands and headed back to the bedroom. Dash met her near the door, freshly dressed and showered. He put his arms around her waist and nuzzled her neck. She laughed. "Well, I *had* made dinner."

"Aww, man," he said, jokingly. He sniffed appreciatively, "It does smell good though." He caught her lips with his own briefly before she entangled herself to make her way to her bureau.

"I need to change. I'm a mess."

Dash plopped himself on the bed, clearly waiting for something. Jaycee grabbed a shirt from the drawer and turned to face him. "This is not dinner and a show."

"How about just the show," he said, laughing and waggling his eyebrows.

Jaycee contemplated him in all seriousness. "I guess you could go grab the bread out of the oven. It'll keep."

Dash took off like a shot, heading towards the kitchen whistling to himself. While he was there, he must've changed the music because soft jazz echoed through the rooms.

Jaycee went into the bathroom and turned on the shower, her jammies now in hand. She poked her head around the bathroom door. "Get yer jammies on, we'll eat in style."

He nodded at her from the bed. "Sounds like a plan."

"I've got something to tell you," she called, leaving the bathroom door open several inches. She stood facing the mirror, staring at her image. She still hadn't undressed yet.

Dash came to the bathroom door and peeked around. "What is it, my little shepherdess."

She turned and faced him, her eyes misting. "We're going to have a baby!"

His eyes grew wide along with his grin. "Not a baby sheep, right? A real baby?"

So much sheep talk had clearly affected his mind. "Yes, a baby-baby," Jaycee said, stamping her foot in mock consternation. "Should be due in February. I saw Dr. Bennett today."

Dash entered the already fogged up bathroom, peeling Jaycee away from the counter and dragging her into the bedroom. "And you've been on your feet all day tending the animals and cooking!"

"I'm not an invalid, Dash. Just goin' to be a momma. Land sakes, Kitty just went through it not two years ago."

"Well, you're my wife, not Colt's and it's time we took some precautions." He turned her around, inspecting her shape. He scowled momentarily and pulled the pliers from her back pocket, holding them up.

"You best not try to put *me* in a pen, Dash Mattheson." She stilled then, staring up at the man she loved with all her heart. She led him to the bed and sat him down. She stood before him, slowly placing a hand on each side of his face. His cheeks were cleanly shaven and he smelled of leather and soap. "Don't let the future overwhelm the moment," she whispered and bent to kiss him as he swept her into his arms.

FROM THE AUTHOR

I hope you enjoyed the *Faith, Love, and Fried Chicken* series. It was my pleasure to bring you the seasons of Jaycee and Dash. And as we part, may I just say my heart is a little bit broader and fuller at having known them and through them, being able to befriend many readers of the series.

Please follow along as I introduce the new *Faith & Fame* series, the first title in the series being *Lainey Sparks*. It's available now at all online retailers. And don't miss the enclosed recipes from all four seasons of *Faith, Love, and Fried Chicken*.

May God bless and keep you and yours.

Love,
Laura

If you liked this book, please help fellow readers by leaving a review at one of the online retailers.

Find Laura with links to sign up for her newsletter and chat with her on social media at

www.LauraJMarshall.com

Jaycee's Momma's Cajun Fried Chicken

Spicy Southern Chicken. Decrease spices by half, as well as tobasco to tone it down, if desired.

Two whole chickens cut up into pieces or precut pieces from store.

2-1/2 cups of flour

2 tsp pepper

2 tsp paprika

2 tsp cayenne pepper

2 tsp onion powder

2 tsp garlic powder

1 egg

1 cup of buttermilk

¼ cup tobasco sauce

Vegetable oil

Fill fryer pan with a couple of inches of oil. Heat to 375.

Mix dry ingredients (flour, pepper, paprika, cayenne, onion powder, and garlic powder) together. Set aside.

Beat egg and add buttermilk. Stir until blended. Add tobasco sauce to this mixture.

Dip chicken into the liquid mixture then dredge into the flour mixture.

Place chicken into the hot oil.

Cook 5-7 minutes per side for smaller pieces and 7-12 minutes per side for bigger pieces.

Remove and drain on paper towels. Salt lightly while hot.

Lemonade Cookies

1 cup butter, softened

3-1/2 cups flour

1 tsp baking soda

¾ cup sugar

2 eggs

1 can lemonade concentrate, thawed, divided

Preheat oven to 400.

Cream sugar and butter until light and fluffy.

Add eggs, one at a time.

Combine flour and baking soda.

Add to creamed mixture, alternating with 2/3 cup of lemonade concentrate and stirring after each addition.

Drop by rounded spoonful onto ungreased baking sheets.

Cook at 400 for 8 minutes.

Remove and place on cooling rack. Brush with remaining lemonade concentrate and sprinkle with sugar.

Allow to cool.

Jaycee's Easy Eggplant Parmesan

2 large eggplants or 3 small, washed and thinly
sliced
6 eggs, beaten
6 cups Italian seasoned bread crumbs
2 medium-sized jars of spaghetti sauce
2 cups grated parmesan cheese (approximately)
Vegetable oil for frying
Paper towels
Salt

Place cut eggplant slices into a bowl of lightly
salted water for one hour. Heat two inches of oil to
350 degrees or until hot. Next, pat slices dry then
dip into egg, then in bread crumbs. Place slices into
hot oil in batches. Flip when underside is browned
(approximately five minutes one side and three
minutes other). Remove to waiting paper towels.
Lightly salt while still hot.
In a 9x13 inch baking dish spread spaghetti sauce
to cover the bottom. Place a layer of eggplant slices

in the sauce. Cover with more sauce and sprinkle with Parmesan cheese. Repeat until pan is full and layered, ending with the cheese.

Bake in preheated 350 degree oven for 35 minutes, or until golden brown.

Momma's Monkey Bread

1/2 cup granulated sugar

1-1/4 teaspoon cinnamon

2 cans (16 oz) refrigerated biscuits (or 4 small cans, if using small, cut biscuits in halves not quarters)

1-1/4 cup firmly packed brown sugar

¾ cup butter or margarine, melted

Bundt pan

Heat oven to 350°F. Lightly grease Bundt pan.

In a large plastic zip bag, mix granulated sugar and cinnamon. (You can also mix in a bowl.)

Separate dough into biscuits; cut each into quarters. Shake in bag to coat or put in bowl of sugar mixture to toss. Arrange around pan. In small pan on your stovetop, melt butter then mix in brown sugar until melted. Pour over sugared biscuit pieces.

Bake 28 minutes or until golden brown and no longer doughy in center. Cool in pan 10 minutes. Turn upside down onto serving plate.

Serve warm.

Jaycee's Shredded BBQ Chicken

Recipe courtesy of Author Precarious Yates

1 TBSP oil

1 small onion, sliced

4 uncooked chicken breasts, whole

Boiling water

1 bottle of your favorite BBQ sauce (we love honey BBQ)

Heat the oil in a cast iron pan or deep skillet over medium heat. Add the onion and cook until translucent. Add the chicken breasts. Once the chicken just begins to sear (turning once), add boiling water until it just covers the chicken. Cover and boil until the chicken has been cooked through (approximately 1 hour). Using two forks, pull apart the chicken while it's in the pan. Allow the chunks and shreds to be different sizes. Add your favorite BBQ sauce and continue to cook (without the lid) until the sauce thickens.

Homemade Ranch Dressing

1 clove garlic

½ teaspoon salt

1/4 cup fresh parsley

2 tablespoons fresh chives

3/4 cup mayonnaise

3/4 cup sour cream

Milk (for consistency)

Cut up one garlic clove. Cover with ½ teaspoon of salt and mash together with a fork. Put in bowl. Finely chop the parsley and chives. Add to bowl along with mayonnaise and sour cream. Stir. Pour in milk a tablespoon at a time while stirring. How much milk depends on consistency desired. Chill for at least an hour.

Shortbread Cookies

4 cups flour

½ teaspoon baking powder

1 pound (4 sticks) butter

1 cup powdered sugar

1 teaspoon vanilla extract

Preheat oven to 350 degrees.

Sift together the flour and baking powder in a bowl
and set aside.

Beat the butter until fluffy then add the powdered
sugar and vanilla extract.

Divide the dough into two separate lumps (loosely
formed) and place in refrigerator to chill for a half
hour.

Using a rolling pin, roll out each piece of dough into
approximately ½ inch thick. Cut the dough into
shapes (I used a round drinking glass tipped upside
down). Place on ungreased cookie sheet. Bake for 8

to 11 minutes. Let cookies sit on sheet for a few minutes before removing to a cooling rack.

Macaroons

3/4 cup flour

14 ounces of coconut shavings

¼ teaspoon of salt

14 ounce can of sweetened condensed milk

 2-1/4 teaspoons of vanilla extract

1 teaspoon water

Grease cookie sheets.

Mix together flour, coconut, and salt. Add milk,

vanilla, and water. Stir well.

Drop by teaspoonful onto cookie sheet.

Bake 20 minutes. Remove from cookie sheets

immediately.

Crockpot Buffalo Chicken Dip

16 ounces of cream cheese (two packages)

1 cup of ranch dressing

½ cup of buffalo style hot sauce

1 cup Monterey Jack cheese

20 ounces of shredded chicken (two cans)

Soften your cream cheese in a warm crockpot using rubber spatula. Add the rest of the ingredients and mix well. Cook the dip in the covered crockpot on high for 1-1/2 hours. Turn to warm and serve with tortilla chips and celery sticks.